I0823635

THE DAUGHTER WHO REMAINS

DAW Books proudly presents
the novels of Nnedi Okorafor

WHO FEARS DEATH

THE BOOK OF PHOENIX

NOOR

BINTI: THE COMPLETE TRILOGY

(Binti | *Binti: Home* | *Binti: The Night Masquerade*
with *Binti: Sacred Fire)*

The Desert Magician's Duology

SHADOW SPEAKER (Book 1)

LIKE THUNDER (Book 2)

She Who Knows

SHE WHO KNOWS (Book 1)

ONE WAY WITCH (Book 2)

THE DAUGHTER WHO REMAINS (Book 3)

THE DAUGHTER WHO REMAINS

BOOK THREE OF SHE WHO KNOWS

NNEDI OKORAFOR

DAW BOOKS
New York

Jacket illustration by Greg Ruth

Jacket design by Jim Tierney

Edited by Betsy Wollheim

DAW Book Collectors No. 1998

DAW Books
An imprint of Astra Publishing House
dawbooks.com
DAW Books and its logo are registered trademarks of
Astra Publishing House

Printed in the United States of America

Library of Congress Cataloging-in-Publication Data

Names: Okorafor, Nnedi author
Title: The daughter who remains / Nnedi Okorafor.
Other titles: DAW books collectors no. 1998.
Description: New York : DAW Books, 2026. |
Series: She who knows ; book 3 |
Identifiers: LCCN 2025036003 (print) | LCCN 2025036004 (ebook) |
ISBN 9780756418991 hardcover | ISBN 9780756419004 ebook
Subjects: LCSH: Okorafor, Nnedi. She who knows (Series)--bk 3 |
LCGFT: Fiction | Science fiction | Fantasy fiction |
Africanfuturist fiction | Novels
Classification: LCC PS3615.K67 D38 2026 (print) |
LCC PS3615.K67 (ebook) | DDC 813.6--dc23/eng/20250901
LC record available at https://lccn.loc.gov/2025036003
LC ebook record available at https://lccn.loc.gov/2025036004

First edition: February 2026
10 9 8 7 6 5 4 3 2 1

Dedicated to fellow witches

Author's Note

Book One of She Who Knows is the story of Najeeba before her daughter Onyesonwu. Herstory in a far future part of Africa, a different time of mysticism and technology. The Before. A teenage Najeeba discovers her mystical gifts and learns how to use them for her own joy and to make her family rich. Then she chooses to bury the gifts deep within herself. The need to be normal is an old one and it rarely leads the not-so-normal to happiness.

Book Two, *One Way Witch,* is the story of what happens to Najeeba and the world directly after Onyesonwu changes everything. For three years, Najeeba is trained by three powerful sorcerers: Aro (first and foremost), Sola, and the kponyungo Sonnn. She emerges a mighty sorceress. She flies into the distant past with Phoenix from *The Book of Phoenix,* who is on her way to change the world. She falls in love with a gifted and spiritually sensitive glassmaker named Dedan. And she faces and overcomes the man who assaulted her, the biological father of her Onyesonwu, the sorcerer Daib.

And so here we are. At the final part of Najeeba's tale. Najeeba has left Jwahir with Dedan to journey across the desert, just as her daughter did years ago in The Before. Where Onyesonwu left on a mission to kill her biological father, Najeeba has also left to kill something terrible—The Cleanser.

Let's see what Najeeba does next . . .

Nnedi

"Let me speak. Do not interrupt me.
I have no time to listen to you."

—Firdaus in the novella "Woman at Point Zero"
by Nawal El Saadawi

CHAPTER 1

Witching

This is the story of how I die . . .

CHAPTER 2

MorningStar

I preferred walking beside MorningStar. The old camel kept a pace that was identical to mine, me with my long legs and she with her smooth, more laid back gait. As the months progressed, she slowed her gait as mine slowed. Dedan would often walk with me, but other times, he rode ahead on Tende. The red-furred camel loved him and Dedan loved him right back. This was no surprise. The way the two found each other was a journey in and of itself. Tende was a beautiful camel and these days, he smelled like desert flowers and dust. He was kind and humorous. And he was strong and just as ready to go where we were going.

Last week, we'd reached the town of Banza. Here, Tende attracted so much attention that we had to leave a day earlier than planned. Banza was a bustling town where the style of dress was very tight. The women wore body-hugging dresses and pants and tops and the men wore body suits that accentuated every bulge. The fabric was thin and treated with weather gel, so no one overheated, but what a refreshing sight it was to see people young to old with pot bellies, stick legs, sagging breasts, and bony backsides proudly sporting the colorful tight bodysuits and dresses.

Dedan and I stayed in the guest house of some of Dedan's relatives. MorningStar and Tende stayed in the camel shed beside the house, and it didn't take the neighbors long to come. Red furred camels like Tende are rare, and he was a beautiful one. By morning, there was a crowd around him. A few camel sellers even approached Dedan wanting to buy Tende. Thus, he spent the whole day at Tende's side, guarding him while politely answering questions. And Tende had growled and spit at anyone who came too close, amusing the crowd even more.

I needed rest and a few good meals, so we stayed. MorningStar slept by our room's window. No one paid her any mind, since she was old and there was nothing extraordinary about her . . . except for the fact that she'd died and I resurrected her by calling back her spirit. The bed was right beside the window and I slept looking up at the stars, knowing that MorningStar was right there.

Those two days in Banza were peaceful. I didn't speak much to Dedan's auntie, uncle, or cousins, other than the brief introductory greeting. They left me alone after that, assuming I needed my rest. Dedan attended a village meeting and two parties without me. The people of Banza like to throw celebrations for every little thing. The first party was for the coming of age of a young cousin who was turning eleven. And the other was for the birth of a white camel. By the second party, his auntie had bought him an outfit to wear to it. The tight body suit accentuated all his best bulges. Since the day he destroyed the glass house, he always wore a leather cord with a blue piece of glass from the glass house around his neck. Clearly his auntie had noticed it, for the body suit was the same vibrant blue as his glass. He'd proudly posed for me in it before leaving.

"Banza-ware always makes me feel like I can do anything," he said.

"As long as you can breathe," I laughed.

I stayed in our room and Dedan brought me heaps of roasted goat meat, grilled vegetables, saffron puff puff, dates, and all kinds of delicacies. I ate these and fed MorningStar and Tende plates of dates Dedan brought them. Afterward, I'd sit on the floor and rise up as the kponyungo, flying the sky for a few hours. I'd return to myself and then sleep. The evening of the fourth day, we moved on. Yes, I rested and ate well, but I was glad to return to the desert. To continue on our way. So was Dedan.

We'd been travelling for eight months. We were strong. We would reach my village Adoro 5 soon enough. But there was something I had to do before turning all my energy, attention, focus, and wrath on The Cleanser.

First, I needed to give birth.

Yes, I was pregnant. I'd been pregnant before I left. Just before. This was not the only reason Aro wanted Dedan and me to leave so soon, but it was one of them.

"You are reckless," Aro had said back in Jwahir, as we stood on the sand dune looking down at the place where Dedan's glass house used to be.

I sighed and shrugged.

"I have known it," he said, frowning. "*But* sometimes, you have to let go of the camel's reigns and let the camel decide if you will live or die." He nodded. "It is tough, but the camel often knows best. And you deserved . . . your happiness. Thankfully, none of us died. I knew the day you conceived. If anything happened, to you, to your baby, to Jwahir, it would have been my fault. I allowed it."

We were quiet, letting the weight of it settle. I wanted to say that I was responsible. He'd warned me over and over about the potential I had to kill us all if I got pregnant while training, yet something wild in me just didn't care. Not about any of it. I'd had sex with Dedan with unbridled abandon. If everyone died, so be it. I'd have killed everyone. Wiped out the past, present, and future of hundreds of people, including Aro, including myself. I risked this without a worry. Irresponsibly. Wholly. Unabashedly. Shamelessly. Brazenly. Impulsively. Willfully. Reckless. But I said none of this.

"What happens now?" I asked.

"Well, the fact that we are all still here is fortunate," he said. "But with all that you are combined with the wonder of life kindled inside you, you could wipe out this entire region just by getting angry. You could rearrange everything by having a bad dream. You could mean to look through time in the bowl of water and instead set the desert on fire. All you need to do is slip. Just once. You are unstable." He pressed his lips together. "I warned you. You don't listen."

"Is it all bad?"

"No," he said. He shook his head. "I don't know. You have to leave here. You know that and you know where you should go."

I nodded. I had something terrible to kill.

"Once you give birth, you will be stable again."

"How can I . . . ?"

"The desert will be good for you. It always has been. It is vast. There is death out there, but there is peace, too. It can contain you. But don't spend more than a week in any towns or villages."

The sun was setting. The last sunset I'd see in Jwahir, I was afraid. I knew.

"When you saw your death, were you pregnant?"

"No."

"Eh heh, good."

We were quiet for a while.

My destination was so distant and so impossible, that all we focused on was the fact that we were leaving. Dedan prepared his glassware shop, I prepared my cactus candy shop. Both practically ran themselves, already. And as for the blacksmithing shop, Jee was happy to take it over completely until I returned. I was brief with him. His unconcealed joy at the news of me leaving was annoying.

That evening, Dedan and I planned a trip to the camel market to buy two camels. However, when I arrived home, I found that we only needed one. MorningStar, the camel I'd brought back to life as part of my training, was standing in front of my house. The old camel had a cowry shell fossil necklace around her neck and there was a printed note placed under a rock in front of my door. "I know you," I said to her as she leaned forward to sniff at me. I patted her cheek and stepped around her to the rock. The note wasn't long.

"Our boy Boho told us how you and the Elder Aro visited our MorningStar. She has been like a new camel ever since. But today, she broke out of her pen and came here. I followed her. She will not leave. She is old. She is home. Sincerely, Oga Bia." I laughed. Aro was respected, but more importantly, he was feared. They had probably wanted to get rid of MorningStar since learning Aro and I had paid MorningStar a visit that day.

"Do you want to see the rest of the world, Morning-

Star?" I asked her. The camel only looked at me. When I went inside and came out with some dates for her, she was still there.

Later than evening, Dedan and I went to the night market. On warm windy nights, the night market became a place where sellers and buyers did their most fruitful business. The combination of the heat, wind, and the sun recently setting energized and excited everyone. Again, luck was on our side because a robust wind began rolling over Jwahir two hours after sunset.

I wore a brown dress that swirled around my ankles as I walked. And I'd unbound my hair to let the wind whip through it. Dedan wore a long white kaftan and he kept laughing every time the wind gusted. People had to make sure their loaves of bread, bowls of spices, woven baskets, stacked capture stations, bottles of scented and cooking oils, displayed paintings, and jars of fresh milk didn't get blown over.

At the camel market, the sellers had to make sure the camels didn't flee. Jwahir's market was nowhere near the size of the one I was used to seeing as a teen, near Adoro 5 back when I sold salt with my father and brothers. Really, the Jwahir camel market had only one seller, the Chiki family. This is the family of

Onyesonwu's closest friend and greatest champion Luyu. However, where Luyu had been female in The Before, she was now male.

Luyu had never returned to Jwahir after she left with my daughter Onyesonwu. I was never able to find out what happened to Luyu, but I suspected the worst. Thus, I'd thought that her presence would simply remain gone in some way, as my daughter in The Now had "died as a young child" to everyone except very few, like Aro. However, Luyu was alive and well and living in Jwahir, the oldest son of the affluent Chiki family. Tall, handsome, flamboyant, in his mid-twenties, he handled most of the selling of the finest camels in the Chiki Camel Mercantile.

I'd seen Luyu a few times at the market and each time . . . he was strange to me. He would stand beside the bread seller, looking around a corner at me. Or he'd be down the road, staring at me. I'd never spoken directly to him. Now here I was with Dedan, walking toward him. The huge zareba was packed with what looked like at least forty grown camels.

"Dedan, you do most of the talking," I said.

He laughed. "Thought you'd want to do it."

I smiled. He was referring to how I'd charmed people into buying salt at the market when I was a teen. "The boy behaves oddly with me," I said. "I think I . . . confuse him."

"Fair enough. No time for tea and coming back the next day for more tea."

"No."

We were feet away. Luyu was talking to two wealthy-looking men in colorful kaftans. One of them laughed and clapped Luyu on the shoulder. They grasped hands. Today, Luyu was wearing a loud yellow kaftan and matching pants. He flashed a winning grin and winked at one of the men. Luyu was stunningly handsome. The wealthy-looking men began to walk away just as Luyu turned to us, still smiling. The moment he saw me, his smile grew, his eyes widened. He took a shaky step back, uncomfortable. Dedan stepped in front of me, holding out a hand.

"I am Dedan."

Luyu shook and slapped the back of Dedan's outstretched hand with the back of his three times. "Luyu," he said.

Around us, the wind gusted and a camel groaned. I stepped up beside Dedan and for the first time since before the world was changed by my daughter, I looked into Luyu's eyes.

"Oga Najeeba," he said, respectfully.

"You know my name?"

"Yes," he said. "And I-I enjoy your cactus candy."

I smiled. He stepped closer. I fought the urge to step back, glancing at Dedan.

"It's funny . . . I . . . I feel like there's something I forgot to tell you," he said. "Because . . ."

"Luyu," Dedan said so loudly that both Luyu and I jumped. "We're here to buy a camel. Not one of your finest; that would be too costly. One who's ready to travel."

"Where are you going?" he asked, but he was still looking at me as he said it.

"West," Dedan said.

"Seven Rivers?"

"Yes."

He held my eyes for a moment longer. Finally, he turned to Dedan, the smile returning to his face. "That's far."

Dedan nodded. "It'll take us . . . months. Depending on the camel."

Luyu cocked his head. "I think I have just the camel for you." He laughed, "But you're going to have to have an open mind about it."

"What do you mean?" Dedan asked.

Luyu put an arm around his shoulder and guided

him up the path through the zareba. "Come. I'll show you."

They chatted as they walked, but I wasn't listening. I stayed several steps behind them, and it gave me a chance to look closely at the camels to my left and right under the dim lights stationed throughout the zareba. Since it was dusty with wind, most of them sat with their long legs folded beneath them, their heads down. Some huddled close to each other and a few didn't seem to care about the wind or dust, happily drinking water or chomping on a large tightly packed brick of alfalfa.

We turned onto a narrower path and walked into a roped off area that was hidden by darkness. I smelled him before I saw him. The stink was so intense that it was almost solid. Rotten, fecal, sweaty, putrid, fermented . . . horrid. I stopped, pinching my nose. "Ugh, what is that," I gasped.

"Shhh," Luyu said over his shoulder. "Just . . . wait."

There was a groan and the sound of high pitched bells, then a splash of water. "Tende," Luyu said softly.

I moved close to Dedan and took his hand, just in time to feel him shudder with revulsion at the smell. Luyu stepped to a lamp and touched it and the area filled with light. Another groan and the slosh of water as a beast continued drinking from a large wooden trough. Its hide was sticky and mucked with sand and dirt, flies buzzing around it, even in the wind. Its powerful legs were covered with something grey and glistening. I squinted, noting something wriggling in the muck on one of its legs. I frowned, realizing, though I should have assumed. "This is a camel?" I asked. The creature's eyes were caked with yellow gunk.

"Yes, his name is Tende."

At the mention of his name a second time, Tende looked back at us, humphed and shook himself out, runnels of saliva slopping from his mouth, dirt rising from his hide into the wind. The wind blew in our direction and some of its spittle hit Dedan. He flinched, shaking it from his hand.

I scrambled back.

Dedan stood his ground, furious. "What is . . . the reason you've brought us to this thing?"

Luyu held up his hands to calm him. "Please . . ."

"We ask you for a reasonably priced camel and you insult us with this diseased creature?" Dedan growled. "This . . . monstrosity?!"

"Why!?" I asked. "Why would you—"

"Please," Luyu begged. "Hear me out."

"What is there to hear?" I asked. "This animal is foul and probably sick."

"He's strong . . . listen. Tende, he's just . . . I don't know where he came from." He looked at me with pleading eyes. "I don't remember. No one does. He stinks, he's cruel, he spits at anyone who tries to clean him . . . and he will not leave. I-I don't show him to anyone, I don't know what to do."

"Why don't you kill it?" I asked.

He shook his head. "No. Never that." He paused. "I don't know why." He took my hands. "I know . . . you're Aro's student." I glanced at Dedan. "Everyone knows," Luyu insisted. "*Please.*" He looked at Dedan. "You built the glass house; that place has healed so many. I have a good friend who can sleep now because of it . . . and you're Najeeba's lover. You both can . . ." He gazed into my eyes with such desperation. "Help."

Dedan and I looked at each other. Then we looked at the beast. It was nasty. Barely a camel. If Luyu didn't know where it came from then it could have been a spirit. Maybe it was sent by something. Or maybe it was just one of those sinister things that should not be, who walked out of the desert and wreaked havoc wherever it went. Best to put it out of its misery. From what Luyu was describing, this creature may have been another who remembered The Before and had in turn kept some of its malice, its disease.

Dedan and I spoke at the same time.

"I can kill it," I said.

"We have to save it," Dedan said.

We stared at each other. I frowned. Dedan approached the camel, Tende.

Dedan is a better person than I.

"Careful," Luyu said. "He spits and he bites."

Dedan nodded, now feet from the camel who'd stopped drinking to look at him, its wet mouth quivering. With rage? Disease?

"Tende," Dedan said.

The camel groaned, stamping a hoof. If it attacked Dedan, I knew how I would kill it. I sat on the ground, my legs stretched before me, ready. Luyu glanced down at me and whispered, "What are you doing?"

"Shhh!" I hissed.

"Do I know you . . . well?" Luyu asked.

"Kind of."

"How?"

"You won't remember." I focused on Dedan. He

was arm's length from the camel. I needed to be ready. As the kponyungo, I would shove the camel's spirit from its body. I could do it within a second, another skill I'd learned over my years with Aro and Sola, though I'd never used it.

"Soft," Dedan whispered. "Softly."

Tende stepped up to Dedan and sniffed his head. I could see Dedan shudder again from the smell. "Okay," Dedan whispered. "Najeeba."

"Yes?"

"Stop preparing to kill this beast," he said. "I think . . . I think I can handle this."

"What?" He was still whispering.

"I think I can handle this," he said a little louder. He slowly turned around. "Luyu, make sure no one gets in our way. No camel, no person. We are leaving."

Luyu nodded. "I will make sure the way is clear! You're taking Tende?"

"Hopefully," Dedan said, calmly. "Tende, will you come?" The camel looked away. "Clear the way."

Luyu rushed off.

Dedan was slowly walking toward me now. And Tende was following him! This stinky, rotting, angry beast of a camel!

"I had a dog once, I think," Dedan said, as he

walked toward me. I turned with him and slowly we began walking up the path. "I dreamed about her. I'm not sure if I did or did not. But I had a dog."

"In The Before."

"I believe so. I've had the dream several times. So I know the details."

"Why haven't you told me about it?"

He shrugged. "Jeeb, it's . . . humiliating to not remember. It's hard to talk about."

I didn't know what to say to this.

"I'd found her in an alley. She was a huge dog, covered in filth and open sores. She tried to bite anyone who went near her. I was only a boy. I wasn't supposed to have a dog. Not any pet. Not any friends. I was only supposed to fill a container with water from the river and bring it back. Instead, I dumped the water on the dog when she tried to bite me. I ran back to the river and got more water. The dog was still there, the water seemed to have calmed her. I dumped water on her again. I was about 8 years old. Water heals everything. That's all I knew. I would swim in the water and my life would seem so perfect . . ."

We were passing the other camels now. Dedan hadn't really had to tell Luyu to clear the way. Everyone, human and camel moved away at Tende's approach.

"The third time I dumped water on the dog, she shook herself out, stepped to a dry spot, curled up and slept. I risked being whipped for not returning swiftly enough, but the dog was so important to me that I was willing to take the chance. The water seemed to have made the dog so much . . . smaller. Not so scary. I gently woke her up and coaxed her to follow me to the river. I was so delighted that she cooperated! There, I washed her. It felt like I worked for hours and hours. I wove a bed for her in a dry protected space in the reeds and later I brought her my dinner, a small piece of meat. She ate it. I knew she would be fine."

We were starting to leave the zareba, the road opening up ahead. Dedan kept talking, "When I came back, she was gone. I never saw her again."

We said goodbye to Luyu, but not thank you. Most people were at the market, so the walk to Dedan's place did not draw a crowd. A few children followed us for a while, pointing and whispering. They knew not to laugh or get too close. Tende followed us to Dedan's home and sat down in his front yard.

"Go home," Dedan said. "I will take care of him."

"Are you sure?" I asked. "I am happy to—"

"Go," he said. "We leave tomorrow in the night. I'll have a long night, then I'll rest."

"What are you going to do?"

"Prepare," was all he said.

I went home to prepare, too. MorningStar needed to drink her water and rest, I would lock up my house, pack my things. But first, I became the kponyungo, and for two hours I thought and worried about nothing but wind, dust, and the stars above.

═══

By the afternoon the next day, I was rested and all packed. I was ready. MorningStar was ready, too. She still sat where she'd been since she'd walked to my house. When I came out, she stretched her head toward me as a greeting. I refilled the tub of water beside her and fed her more alfalfa and dates. Then I went to see how Dedan was doing.

Jwahir was in full swing, and I was tempted to stop by my cactus candy shop. However, I'd already said goodbye to Gisma and Makka. I didn't have any urge to check on my husband's blacksmithing shop.

The walk to Dedan's house took twenty minutes, and by the time I reached his road, I was sweating. The day was very hot and its heat felt good; it is the kponyungo in me. So I arrived at Dedan's house smiling. I slowed as I approached. There was a small crowd of people standing on the road looking into his yard. I was reminded of how people behaved with his glass house.

"What's going on?" I asked an old man who was walking away. His name was Bior and I knew him well.

"Ah, Najeeba, fascinating, just fascinating," was all he said, as he shuffled on.

"Wait, where are you going?"

"To get my wife! She'll definitely want to see this."

I ran to Dedan's house. I pushed through the people standing there. For all its past flaws, Jwahir is a wonderful place with wonderful people. Case in point, not one person stepped onto Dedan's property, despite their intense curiosity. Thus, once past the crowd, I was free to walk up to Dedan and Tende slowly, taking it all in.

"Have you . . . slept?" I asked, pressing my hands to my cheeks.

"Some." He laughed and fiddled with the blue glass of his necklace.

I stood there, staring. He must have worked

through most of the night. He must have pulled gallons and gallons of water from the night sky with his capture station . . . because it had to have taken a *lot* of water to wash Tende. And not just water. "How?" I asked.

"I ran back to the market after you left. The soap seller Khamis, he is a friend and he knew what I needed. He brought me brushes, combs, rough bark, a stack of giant aloe vera leaves, and calabashes of this melon castile soap. It smells beautiful. Khamis helped me some, once he was sure Tende was safe to be around. At first, Tende wasn't. He kept trying to bite us and spat at Khamis five times! Eventually, we got him to calm down. Khamis left after an hour. I did most of it. Washed and washed and washed him for most of the night. He let me." He paused, looking at Tende. "By morning, when the sun came up, Tende dried. And I saw . . . oh Ani, I saw that he'd *transformed.*"

Last night, Tende had been a stinking, rotting, oily, dirt monster. Now, he was a magnificent red furred camel with piercing black eyes. *This* was what people were staring at. There were a few patches of raw skin, but mostly, Tende looked like a creature from a folktale who walked out of the desert as a reward for the story's hero. Dedan walked over to Tende and patted his long neck and the camel vibrated deep in his throat.

Dedan was no sorcerer, but there was such sensitivity to him, a mysticism about him that he'd clearly been born with. I suspect it was there in The Before. Dedan had truly, deeply washed Tende. I slowly approached. "Is it okay?" I asked.

Dedan nodded. "For you, yes." He motioned to the people watching. "For them, absolutely not. Thankfully, they know it."

I stepped up to Tende and locked eyes with him. I was still ready to take his life if he tried anything. Maybe he knew that, maybe he didn't care. He brought his large head close and humphed hard enough to blast air in my face. "Yes, well, I'm not afraid of you either," I said. I held up a hand. "I am Najeeba. I'll be travelling with you."

He sniffed me and then turned to Dedan who'd brought him some dates to eat. The camel ate them right out of his hand, grunting with pleasure the entire time, while keeping an eye on me.

"Aro would say, 'Unexpected, but expected,'" I said.

═══

Now, eight months later, I'd come to know both camels well. MorningStar was a good good friend. She was loyal, loving, and protective of me, even stomping on a snake that had gotten too close to me one night. She was strong, despite the fact that she was old.

Tende was also strong, always ready to go even after long days of walking through the night and early morning. And not surprisingly, even when the wind became dusty, his coat stayed clean. Tende and Dedan were so close that Dedan claimed they sometimes shared each other's dreams.

"What does he dream about?" I'd asked.

"Running through fields of lush green plants," he said. "We both love that dream!"

The last eight months, as I grew heavier and heavier with the baby, we'd all been happy. We are moving toward something terrible, but we are therefore moving toward answers. And camels like to travel.

I destroyed nothing. I killed no one except several desert hares, the occasional bird, lizards, and aku that we ate. I often walked off alone over the dunes where I became the kponyungo and explored ahead.

In this way, we needed no map, and I knew which towns were safe for us to spend a few days in and which to avoid.

I continued to study and hone all the skills Aro taught me. This was risky, considering my pregnancy, but it was a risk I had to take. I needed to be able to do what I needed to do when the time came. I didn't know how I would do it yet, but I knew that I needed to have all the pieces to put the puzzle together. Many of those pieces were the skills Aro, Sola, and the great kponyungo Sonnn taught me. All the Mystic Points, from the Mmuo Point to the Uwa Point to the Alusi Point. If I were ever ready, I would wield the Okike Point, the Creator, "the point that cannot be touched".

I avoided witches. I wasn't sure why, but my instincts told me to do so. For now. While I carried my child. Witches unleashed me, there was no control while around them. This was why I loved them, but also why they would make me especially dangerous in my condition. Plus, it wasn't the time to have my body whisked into the air and slammed to the ground. Still, when things were quiet, and Dedan and the camels were asleep, I walked a few feet away and drew my favorite juju symbol in the sand. The "hawk," the essence of controlled, intentional, ambitious flight. If I were feeling weighed down by memory, sadness, time, pain, this would chase it away and leave my mind light enough to enjoy flight.

Dedan spent a lot of time collecting glasslike stones we occasionally came across as we walked, polishing them and constructing temporary pyramids with them when we camped. He'd also fill with water a small pitcher that he'd bought at a market to make intricate sand sculptures. He'd wet the sand and build towers and sculpt shapes with it. And when he finished, before it dried completely, he'd bring Tende to stomp on it.

Dedan and I talked as we walked. About everything and nothing. The sound of our voices a narrow song in the desert. Other times, we were quiet for days. Tende and MorningStar were like auntie and nephew. They argued at times. MorningStar always ate first. And on cool nights, they snuggled warmly, MorningStar's murmuring like a lullaby. We never starved or went thirsty. If any of us was ill, it was brief and eventually passed. Our capture stations kept us all hydrated and cool and even allowed us to bathe.

Yes, happiness. And peace. No uncontrolled, ruinous destruction. And we had direction and purpose. I knew where we were going. What a time those months were. So when I saw the massive wall of dust in the distance and I felt the wetness of my water breaking between my legs, despite having two weeks to go, I wasn't surprised. Happiness always leads me to the dark.

CHAPTER 3

Red

A place being dark does not mean it is empty. Sola once told me this during my training when I complained that I couldn't even find peace in my deepest sleep. His words didn't bother me much until that night when I was trying to sleep and I realized what was making me restless was that I didn't feel quite alone in the darkness behind my eyes.

The darkness can often be more occupied than the light. Heavy. Weighted. Warm. Strong. Breathing on the back of your neck. All while you cannot see what it is doing. That sense of dread was what I felt as I withered to the sand, the pain of labor gripping me. I felt terribly powerful.

"Dedan," I said. "The baby is coming."

He was looking at the sky. A wall of dust was gliding toward us. A greater witch. We had endured dust storms before. We had a method. It was a good one and it worked. But this storm was a big one.

"Right now?!" he shouted, as he yanked the brown stretchy cloth from the pack Tende carried. He shook it out. We'd bought it in Banza, where tight stretchy durable material was common. It had been my idea. The cheapest cloth was one dyed a rich deep blue using *nil,* an indigo plant. Once back in the desert, I'd worked a protective charm on it so that it could withstand and repel the heavy winds of dust and sand storms.

This cloth was yards wide and long enough to have the camels sit on it while it ballooned over us. We'd practiced and then done this several times now, and Tende and MorningStar knew the routine. And before I knew it, we had a makeshift shelter of the bright blue cloth over us. On one side, Tende sat on the cloth and Dedan pulled the section under Tende and firmly fastened it to a notch on his saddle. On the other side, MorningStar sat with the same type of setup.

In the center, I lay on the sand aching from the contraction that had hit me minutes ago. I could hear the storm. It was close, about to roll over us any minute. I didn't need to see the sky to know.

"Are you all right?" Dedan asked.

I shook my head. We stared at each other, neither of us wanting to speak what was on our mind, that this was a bad omen. There was no way to gather water using the capture station. All we had was a small bag of it. Barely enough to wash the baby if I gave birth. If he arrived. If she arrived. I didn't know. I had tried to look inside myself to find out, but this baby didn't speak to me as Aro said a child conceived during training might.

"Do you want some water?"

"No."

"What do you need?"

"I don't know," I whispered.

"Is it like the first time?"

"That was a long time ago."

"Over twenty years," he said.

We both laughed. He took my hand. "This isn't how it happens," he reminded me. Yes, I'd told him that I'd seen my death as part of my initiation.

Amazingly enough, Dedan's words worked. I nodded, calmed.

My ears popped. Tende and MorningStar seemed to feel it, too. Tende put his head down and MorningStar groaned deep in her throat. "It's here," I said. The cloth protecting us rippled and then began to shudder. Dedan and I looked up at it. The howl of the great witch was terrible, deep and wide. The camels groaned some more and now MorningStar put her head down, too. Between them, Dedan and I grasped each other tightly, and I shut my eyes.

Another contraction took me. My belly seized up. The combination of the storm outside and the one inside my body made me feel as if something powerful snatched me in its arms and squeezed. Squeezed me so hard that before I understood what was happening, I shot out of my body. I burst upward in a blaze, right through the cloth. And suddenly, I was in chaos. Brown motion all around me, moving in a thousand different directions at once.

It would have torn me apart. Scattered me until I was nothing. But I was the kponyungo and the wind did not harm me when I burst through the cloth into the open. I caught myself, took a breath, noting the lightness of being outside of my body's labor. I turned and flew through the cloth, back to myself. But when I tried to reenter, something kept me out. I tried again. It was as if a solid barrier were there. I looked like I was sleeping. Dedan was speaking softly to me. "Don't worry. Don't worry. Don't worry."

I roared with rage, trying to reenter myself again.

Suddenly, Dedan looked up, right at me. His face full of distress. Tears in his eyes. "I will take care of you! If you have left, don't worry! I will be the labor!" He paused, breathing heavily. "Go see if there is help nearby!"

I left. His words. Him giving me orders. This aligned me and kept me from just staying there and roaring and losing my mind. He'd known. He knew me well. Oh he knew me so well. It is good to have someone who knows you well. Who loves you for what he knows.

I flew into the storm. This time, the great witch didn't scare me. I had purpose. I didn't need direction. First I flew upward. The howl and shriek of the great witch and then the sudden silence as I burst into the blue sky, the midday sun. I looked down at the great witch– a thick brown orange snake, coiling about itself, blanketing the desert with its girth. A beauty and a horror. It had an eye. That eye looked no bigger than a mile or two. And in that eye, where the air was free of dust, the rest of the storm rotating around it like a hurricane, were what looked like houses. People?

Praise Ani, I thought, in awe. *We have found them.* I flew down.

"The Vah? They . . . exist?" I'd asked back in Jwahir when Aro told me he thought we should find them. My mother used to tell me stories featuring the Vah, more commonly known as the Red People, when I was a small child. The idea of people with red brown skin who lived in a nomad village of Ssolu protected by a dust storm was wonderfully ridiculous to my young mind. In my mother's stories many adventurers were blown away trying to get to the Vah because it was believed that they carried a great treasure.

"Only one adventurer was able to make it through the storm alive and only because he was lucky. The storm's wind had whisked him into the air and dumped him right in the middle of Ssolu, the Red People's village. One of his legs was broken, but he did not care. He'd made it. Done the impossible. He got up and hobbled around for hours, searching and searching for the treasure. All he found were happy people with brown skin that had a red hue because it was rubbed with palm oil. Eventually, a family asked him to lie down in their tent because they saw he was exhausted.

They set his leg in a cast. They gave him food and water. The children sang to him. The parents asked him where he was from. He slept. Eventually, he was able to walk with no pain. And no one from his own village ever saw him again."

At this point, I'd always feign fear and shock and ask why no one ever saw him again. Did they kill him? Throw him to the wind? Would his bones fly forever in the storm? And my mother would only smile knowingly and then say, "That's the end of the story." As I got older, when I considered the story, I understood it. The adventurer didn't want to be found. It was a story that stayed with me, but as a metaphor for the all-encompassing and transformative power of happiness. I never imagined it was a story about a people who actually existed.

"The Vah exist, Najeeba," Aro had said. "And Sola and I believe they will be able to help you if you can find Ssolu, their moving village protected by a dust storm."

Over the months, as Dedan and I travelled west to my town in the Seven Rivers Kingdom, I didn't know how we would find a people who lived in a nomadic village in the center of a sandstorm. I couldn't get my mind around it, so I didn't try. Sometimes what you didn't know how to find found you.

When I got closer, I saw that the homes were large and sturdy goat skin tents. This had to be Ssolu. There was nearly a mile of open space between the beginning of the village and the storm. I decided to stay back and fly around it, keeping close to the edge. I could see that people were out and about, none venturing beyond the last tent. They all wore variations of red garments and from what I could see, their skin was indeed a rich brown red. And they could *see* me!

A child stopped and pointed. Then a group of women. Some men. Word spread quickly and within a minute, people began to rush to the village's edge to look. From all parts! How were they communicating? Did they have networked portables? Their curiosity grew so intense that I took a chance. I went toward the village.

I flew low toward the men and women. They didn't flee; a few frowned at me, one pointed, most simply looked interested. What exactly were they seeing? A kponyungo? If so, they weren't afraid at all. I soared feet above them, and I heard a woman hiss something at me as she reached up. Now I was over their tents! I slowed for a better look. I could smell food frying. There was a warmth here.

I changed to my human form and stood between two tents. I knew where I wanted to go because I'd seen it up ahead. I wanted to arrive there on foot. It was a tent like all the others, but with my kponyungo eyes I saw a bright light dribbling from it like mist. As I walked, a few people saw me and moved away. No one spoke to me. Waiting for me at the tent were a tall red-brown woman with a bald head and an old man whose wrinkled red brown face reminded me of wind and sand.

"I need help," I said.

"Where are you?" the man asked.

"In the storm."

He nodded and looked at the tall woman. "I told you."

The tall woman looked annoyed. "Which way have you come from?"

"East. I . . . am about to have my baby."

She rushed away.

"Ah. Now I understand," the old man said. He stepped closer to me. "You don't have much time."

"What do you mean?"

But it was as if his words were juju because something yanked me back. I was tumbling and soaring. I burst through a tent, having only a moment to meet the eyes of a woman with long black braids before passing right through her. She shrieked, but I was already moving again. I was pulled upward, first into the clear sky, then back into the dust storm. Orange-brown windy chaos. Then I was falling toward a brown bubble, battered by the winds. I slammed into my body with such force, I thought I would pass right through myself into the depths of the Earth.

The pain of a contraction wrapped itself around all my senses. I bucked and shrieked.

"Jeeb!?! Breathe, my love, breathe!" Dedan shouted, leaning down to touch my face. His voice was shaky, his face wet with sweat and tears. It felt like a thousand degrees under the quaking cloth.

"HURTS!" I screamed as the contraction tore through me. I grabbed his hand and squeezed as hard as I could. When it finally let up, I looked at him, terrified. "I . . . I think they are coming."

"What? Who?"

Outside, it grew calm. The cloth stopped undulating, slowly settling on top of us. Tende raised his head and groaned. MorningStar shook her head and began to rise. "Wait," Dedan said, but she wasn't waiting. Blown by a powerful cooling wind, the bright blue cloth flew over Tende's head. Tende in turn stood up tall, too. Dedan jumped to his feet, looking up at the clear blue sky. "Ani is great!" he whispered.

I wasn't looking up. I was looking across the sands. They were about a quarter of a mile away. And they came from all directions. The Vah. The Red People. The villagers of the nomad village Ssolu. Even the Nuru feared them; Nuru stories only involved the Vah as evil sorcerers and violent nomads corrupted by the desert's mysticism. Aro insisted that they were simply a nomadic people who lived away and outside of everyone else. Free and strange. And they were believed to naturally know and even *work* juju. That was why they were not afraid of my kponyungo form, it was normal to them.

Sola had said one of their sorcerers was a friend of his. Even with all this, I had not quite believed either of them. And then when Aro told me to find them, that they could help me with my baby . . . if I lived, I put it out of my head. At the time, we had a long way to go and I was focused on leaving, and later, killing The Cleanser. The myth of the Red People was a nice idea to travel toward. Now it was time to look the idea in the face.

They were close now. There were about twenty of them, so it certainly wasn't the whole village. They wore blood red garments, loose and billowing, pants, dresses, skirts, kaftans, several covered their faces with veils as protection from the dust. They rode and walked beside their camels. Their camels had blood red saddles and adornments. A plump short girl who wore no veil walked faster than everyone. She was coming right toward me. She shouted something just as a contraction ripped through my body.

"What do we do? What do we do?" Dedan said, grabbing his necklace.

"Ahhh! Nothing, nothing," I groaned.

"Okay," he said, breathlessly. He scrambled to his things and reached into his garments, and I hoped he wasn't trying to find his machete. I writhed, shutting my eyes, tears pouring from them. The pain was like something hot and electric seeping into my skin, pouring into my mouth, creeping into my nostrils, oozing into my ears, burning my vagina. But also blooming from within me . . . where a wild seed had germinated and grown.

I didn't give my baby too much of my thoughts.

Let me pause in my telling of all this for a moment. Let me talk about my baby. The moment I knew I was pregnant, the first thing I felt was . . . intense power. Life was kindled inside me. For years, I'd worked with Sola and Aro. I'd learned and practiced deep mysteries. I'd conversed with masquerades. I'd lived in the wilderness with kponyungo. I'd walked the desert. My love had died. My daughter had saved the world. I was a hero to my*self*. But when life bloomed in me this second time, it was as the Okike Point, the Mystic Point of the unknown, the most powerful point, had touched me. And it's touch was . . . delicate, careful, focused. The second thing I felt was joy.

"Onyesonwu," I'd whispered. "I wish you could know about this." I had been in my bed in my house. Dedan was not there that morning. The sun was shining through my window. I was wearing a thin nightshirt. I'd turned so that the sunbeam was shining on my face. That's when I realized I was pregnant. I'd hugged myself, pressing my hands to my belly. I was in my own soft bed, not in a tent alone in the desert. Forty-two years old, not twenty years old. I was pregnant because of love, not because of hate. I wept. Oh I wept. And then I laughed.

"How times have changed," I'd said. Then I was

afraid. I remembered the woman Aro told me about. The woman who'd wiped out her entire town, or so the story went. I was not sure I believed it. It didn't sound like something I should believe. Aro was still Aro and even great people have flaws. I had known Aro's flaw even before he started training me. He had a problem with girls and women. However, there are always kernels of truth in stories like the one he told me.

I kept my pregnancy a secret from Aro. I continued with my training. I was thorough, careful, I studied and practiced harder. I walked with greater care. Everything I did had to be perfect. And when it couldn't be, I braced myself for the end, for the destructive, the unpredictable. I operated with this fear for two weeks, and then Aro figured it out. But it was another week before he told me. He told me that he'd watched me closely, and suffered the same fear as me. Existential dread. Whatever happened now would be his fault, now that he knew and did nothing to stop my training.

"I told Sola," he said, two days before he would tell me to leave. "He laughed. Then he said, 'She will destroy us all . . . if you don't send her away. Ah, women. They are change.'"

Power. Joy. Fear. This was larger than me. Larger than what I wanted. My baby was a question mark. Boy or a girl. Healthy or sickly. Normal or heavy with mystery. I didn't know what to expect. I had no warning. I hoped the Vah understood that they should stay away from me. I wanted to tell Dedan to leave me, too. I *was* dangerous. I knew it. I was a sorcerer, and I was a potent one. I'd known this since I was a child and now I was coming into my greatest strength. Right there in the sand, after my water broke.

"L . . . leave me," I grunted. But the small girl of about ten was kneeling beside me, grinning.

"I'm Eyess," she said in rich Okeke. "I see you. You're coming with ussssss."

The tall woman I'd seen in the village shoved the girl aside and pushed her face to mine and touched my arm. She was sweaty, dusty, and her eyes were twitching. Her breath was hot and smelled like smoke. "You've put us all in danger by coming here," she hissed. She was a sorcerer like me. Her name was Ting.

I could only gag as another contraction hit me. The people surrounded me, some were women, some were men. I was lifted and a soft, clean, red blanket was placed beneath me. They set me down on it. Then Ting took over, barking orders, telling two men to boil hot water, another to fetch soft cloth, telling three women and one man to sing soft words.

Then she was in my face again. "Don't you dare go elu. Your baby *needs* you to stay. Take the pain!" She kept shouting, hissing at me, as the contractions rolled over me. She was terrifying. I *did* want to leave. When I'd had Onyesonwu, it was like something pushed me aside and focused me, did the work, took the pain. I didn't have to be in it. This time, I was fully present and the pain left me scattered and flailing for any control.

Dedan stayed by my side. He held my hand, but said nothing. Over hours, as my labor pains intensified and came faster, a village grew around me. The Vah moved from where they'd been and set up with me at the center. The tent where I'd met the two sorcerers while in my spirit form, the tall woman whose name was Ting and the old man named Ssaiku, was now feet away. The storm whipped back up to hide the village. I was aware of none of this at the time.

Night fell, or so I later realized.

═══

The pain blurred time.

═══

Ting told me to push. I pushed. Breathed. I was outside and above, the eye of the storm revealed a sky full of stars. The contractions rolled over me and I shut my eyes. Ting told me to push. I pushed. I was silent in my focus. As always, I was not alone in the darkness behind my eyes. Dedan pressed his head to mine, his hands pressing my shoulders. The men and women around me hissed with my efforts and it felt like they were adding wind beneath my wings, "Sssssssssssss!"

I pushed harder and . . . felt something rupture. Then I felt a release as she flew from me. Decades ago, my first daughter Onyesonwu had come out fast and shrieking; I vaguely even recall hearing her holler muffled before she hit the air at full pitch. She was screaming before she came into the world! My second daughter came into the world quiet as an owl in flight. She shot right into Ting's hands. Dedan cut the cord, two men helped as Ting washed the child. Throughout, I just watched through the rainbow haze of my pain and fuzziness of my exhaustion, still silent. My child looked around with wide brown eyes. A new-born isn't supposed to be able to focus. She was breathing calmly, she was strong. Swathed in a soft red cloth, Dedan placed her in my arms.

I still needed strength to expel the afterbirth, but I managed to meet her dark brown eyes. And her eyes met mine. Striking. Stunning. She looked at Dedan who was kneeling beside me. "She reminds me of the sunshine through the glass house," he said.

"She swept in like the wind," I said. I paused, remembering the word the kponyungos liked to call each other when they played, when they were happiest. Speaking the word itself was like exhaling a breath. "Ikuku. Let's name her Ikuku. It means 'wind'."

"Ikuku," he said, narrowing his eyes. "It's a juju name."

I smiled. It was. "Will you name her?"

"You've already named her." He shook his head. "I couldn't choose anything stronger than that."

"Ikuku is a good name," I sighed, shutting my eyes.

He kissed my forehead. "I'll protect you and The Wind for as long as I'm alive and after I'm dead."

I took and squeezed his hand, his closeness giving me strength. I smiled. "You've just given her a nickname."

"I have? Oh, maybe I did." He touched her cheek. "Let me hold The Wind. You sleep."

I shut my eyes as he took her away. I could hear him telling the others, "She is Ikuku. We've named her Ikuku." I slept and when I woke, I was in a tent on a soft red pallet, and my skin had been moisturized with an oil that smelled of dried flowers and crushed leaves. Ikuku was sleeping beside me in a basket. I didn't know where Dedan was.

The first thing I did was check my body. My belly felt heavy and stretched. If I moved, my privates burned, but not as much as hours ago. My stomach was empty. And I felt muscle-sore all over. I glanced at Ikuku again. She was sleeping deeply. I shut my eyes and held my arm to my nose and took a whiff of the wonderful oil coating my skin. I imagined green vines slowly growing in patches, beneath desert stones, just after a rare rain. The tiny flowers opening to drink the sunshine and attract pollinators. Picked by old women who ventured out into the desert right after the rain. Women who knew exactly where to find the flowers. They took the buds and the leaves, but only half, because they knew the plants needed to live for the next rain.

I settled. The oil was soothing, but also healing. I

opened my mouth and exhaled quietly. Then I was above my body as the kponyungo. I coiled in on myself as I hovered above Ikuku, looking at her with my kponyungo eyes.

Things were always clearer and more vibrant when I was the kponyungo. I could see the layers and separation. And sometimes I could see atmosphere. Ikuku was not a large or small baby. She was healthy, but not plump. She had a round head, large eyes and thick pink lips. She was a rich brown and had a darker brown birthmark on her left thigh. She had a head full of lush black hair. She was a beautiful normal child.

She cracked opened her eyes and gazed into mine. And she didn't take her eyes off me. I floated to the left and right and she turned her head to follow me. She fidgeted and burbled, but she didn't cry. I moved closer and still she watched.

"Okay, Ikuku," I said. I turned and flew off.

When I returned, they were not calling her Ikuku or The Wind. The Red People, the Vah, the inhabitants of the village known as Ssolu had decided to name my child. In Ssolu, news travels quickly. Their indigenous language is made to be heard over the noise of an always present dust storm. This is the origin of Ssufi, a language that consisted of mostly S's and sh's and whistles, sounds with a higher frequency and pitch.

I'd been gone for an hour and in that time, people learned of Ikuku's healthy birth. They talked about her round head and the fact that she didn't damage my body on her way out. They said she looked like her father, but she acted like her mother who was a sorcerer. But what they talked about most was that she was a child of their dust storm yet she was born calm and controlled. They loved that. So they did not call her by her name, Ikuku. They didn't call her by her father's nickname, The Wind. They called her Sssolu, an enunciation of the village's name.

When I returned to myself, I found that Ting was sitting on a chair looking at me. She began telling me all this as I sat up. "The extra 'S' marks her as the sound of Ssolu, she is the village's roar," Ting continued.

I scoffed. "Why won't anyone allow me to name my child?"

"In Ssolu, a child belongs to the village," she said. "It is normal. Motherhood is deeply respected and understood, so there is no ego." She patted my shoulder.

I grunted.

"Seems like you have lots of ego," she said.

"I am a woman who knows the importance of taking up space."

"That's fair," Ting said. "How are you feeling?"

"Better."

"Good."

"Where is my daughter?"

"Dedan has her. I don't know where he is."

Satisfied with this, I took the moment to really look at Ting. Her head was mostly bald and she wore large golden earrings. Like all the Vah people, her flawless skin was supple with the signature red palm oil they all used. Her nails were long, strong and sharp. She wore a long loose red sleeveless dress that showed her muscled arms. There were nsibidi tattoos on her biceps and on the swells of her breasts. They were akpambe, a type of nsibidi used to smell out any type of juju. She must have known I was coming days ago.

"So . . . are you going to tell me who you are?" I asked.

"I'm Ting."

"I know that."

"I'm a sorceress."

I laughed at the feminine phrasing. "I assumed. And the elder? Is he your teacher?"

"Yes. He is Ssaiku. Our village chieftess is Sessa, our chief is Usson. You will meet them when you are ready."

"My teacher is Aro," I said.

The pleasant look dropped from her face. She stood up. Her shocked look became one of understanding. She pressed her hands to her chest as she gasped. She stumbled back. "Aro?"

"Yes," I said, frowning. "What . . . what's wrong? He told us to find you." I stood and my body screamed. I ignored it. "What is it?"

She took more steps back. She was almost out of the tent. "Who are you?" she asked.

I scowled. "My name is Najeeba. You already know, I'm a sorcerer."

"But . . ." She stepped closer now, her eyes wide. She came up to my face. "*Who* are you?"

I looked her in the eye. We stared at each other. Her eyes began to flood with tears. "Do . . . you remember?"

I didn't know who she was talking about. "Ting, I just gave birth. I barely remember my own name."

"I see her," she whispered. "I see her in your eyes.

You may not, but I remember her." She beat her fist against her chest. "*I* will never forget her."

I blinked. "Onyesonwu?"

"You are her mother."

I nodded. My body was vibrating. I clenched my fists. What was this?

"You remember," she said, grasping my hands tightly. She had big strong hands. It hurt. I welcomed this, she was steadying me.

"Everything," I gasped.

"The way things were?"

"The Before."

"Does your man?"

I shook my head. "Does your teacher?" I had to work hard to remember his name. "Ssaiku?" She held me by the shoulders. I was quivering so much, she was holding me up now.

She nodded. "Only him," she said. "No one else. So it is only sorcerers who remember, then."

"I wasn't a sorcerer when it happened," I said.

"You are her mother, maybe it was that for you . . . and that you would become a sorcerer."

I shrugged. " I don't know." I took a deep breath, steadying myself.

"Aro was her teacher."

"Yes. And mine."

"I knew her, Najeeba."

I felt a wave of dizziness and she held my shoulder tighter. "How?" I asked.

"I knew all of them, your daughter and her friends. They were here for a time." Ting sat down in front of me. "I saved her from her father's cruel poison curse. I gave her nsibidi. On each arm."

I leaned on her and shut my eyes as I put it together. I had been in Ssolu before. At the time, I had not cared *where* Onyesonwu was. I'd barely noticed the dust storm I passed through to get to her. I hadn't questioned anything. I'd only wanted to see my Onyesonwu one last time. That day, I'd appeared to her as the kponyungo and she'd, in turn, changed into one. We'd flown together.

"She was afraid," Ting said. "But she knew she would do it. She knew she could do it. Ah, I can see so clearly that you are her mother."

I was tired. So tired.

"Are you looking for . . . ?"

"No," I quickly said. "She's gone."

"Could your——"

"No. Ikuku is not Onyesonwu."

"You're sure?"

"There will only ever be one Onyesonwu, and there is only one Ikuku. I am not . . ." I sighed. "I have come from the East for another reason."

Ting helped me back onto my mat. She stood back, looking down at me. "You need to rest. We can finish talking later." She left me alone.

I named my second daughter Ikuku. Her father nicknamed her The Wind. But she was Sssolu. The village not only named her, they *claimed* her. Even Dedan and I began to call her Sssolu. It was a beautiful name and as all things the Vah spoke, the name rolled off the tongue and it carried.

The Vah's culture was fascinating. The Mystic Points were in their DNA. They did not believe in monogamy, but were fiercely compassionate, empathetic and loyal. Though they had Okeke facial features and hair texture, their skin was a rich red brown from the palm oil they rubbed into it. The Vah were neither Nuru nor Okeke. Not even Aro knew what their origins were. I often wondered if there was a book about them in the Paper House of my village or one of the other Adoro villages. If there were, it would be considered a book of secrets.

We'd been there ten days, the longest we'd stopped anywhere. After spending a quiet five hours nursing Sssolu while Dedan lay at our feet daydreaming, Dedan took her, and I went to find Ting. The walk made me feel good, despite my residual pain and sore muscles. I stopped in a space between two large tents and paused. I stretched my back and looked up at the sky. I grinned. After nine months, I was finally alone in my body again, a surprisingly refreshing feeling.

I asked around and was directed to the outskirts of the village. Once you got beyond the last tents, everything became what all things eventually became—so much sand. It was fine and nearly white here. The great witch that protected the village churned and roiled a mile away, simultaneously brown and shadow. Her roar was unbridled here. You could always hear her in the town, but this close, with no tents holding it back, with no juju dampening it, she allowed nothing to out-scream her.

Despite the noise, the wind here was gentle. I understood why Ting came out here to meditate. It was peace in proximity to unbridled chaos. People like us found comfort in places like this. She sat in the sand, her long legs stretched before her, leaning back on her elbows.

"Ting," I said, when I reached her. I didn't shout over the noise, and she heard me.

"Sit down."

I did.

"Move closer."

We were shoulder to shoulder, close enough to not have to yell. I noted another thing about the Vah that I found a bit annoying. They were a close people.

"How are you feeling?" she asked.

I nodded. "Good."

"I have never given birth. I am always amazed by how women survive it."

"Oh, it can't be the most amazing thing you've seen being a sorceress."

"It's not, but it's still amazing."

We gazed at the chaos for a while. It was hypnotic and soothing. Very different from the way it was when I flew through it as the kponyungo. Nothing soothing about that.

"Why?" she asked.

"Why what?"

"Why did you leave home to travel West? Most

travel East. And *you* remember everything, so you have no unresolved . . . feelings."

"I don't." I sighed. "I came here to tell you why."

"Because you want to leave soon, I know."

I did want to leave. I hadn't spoken this to Dedan. I suspected he'd be angry. "If we don't leave here now, we'll be here for months, or even longer," I said. "I . . . I love it here."

"Dedan has been going to the men's meetings. He's captivated everyone with his stories about his glass house. Plus, his skills as a glassmaker are needed here."

I hadn't known any of these things.

"There are several women who will want to share him with you."

I bristled. This, I knew.

"There is something I need to kill," I said.

"Is it alive?"

I looked at her. This wasn't the question I expected. "I don't know."

"Can it die?"

"I will make it so."

"How do you know you need to kill it if you don't really know if it's alive? Do you even know *what* it is?"

I didn't answer. I didn't. "It's called The Cleanser."

Her eyes grew wide. "Ayyy! I have heard of it! It is a thing amongst the Osu-nu.".

I told her as much as I could. How my father's sister had been taken by The Cleanser when she was fourteen and how they were never very close again. How his sister had grown into a beautiful and mysterious young woman with many men who wanted to marry her. I told her how the Nuru killed my father's family because of his sister's forbidden love. I told her of my own classmate who'd been taken by The Cleanser and how she, too, grew to be beautiful and sought after. I told her about the grimy piece of paper I'd once seen when I was a teen that said something about The Cleanser on it, otherwise there was nothing. Just myth, hearsay, glimpses and acceptance.

I told her about how I'd been fully aware when Onyesonwu did what she did and things went from The Before to The Now. Lastly, I told her about how, not long after, I'd left my body and travelled West as the kponyungo and seen The Cleanser with my Kponyungo eyes. How I'd flown over it and truly *seen* it and then been sure that I had to kill it.

When I stopped talking, she got to her feet. "Let's walk," she said. "I need to move my body. This is a lot to process. Oh, I'm sorry . . . are you okay to walk?"

I slowly got up, feeling every ache. I nodded. "It will do me good, too."

"What is it like to be the kponyungo? I can't change the way you can and your daughter could. Onyesonwu said Aro could, as well. Sola, too, I remember."

"Sola was here?"

"Sola knows Ssaiku well. They're old friends. I don't know what those two got up to in the past. I have never asked. Ssaiku is much older than he looks."

"Sola, as well," I said. "He is also my teacher. I've had three teachers." We were walking past a large tent to our left, the storm a mile to the right. I slowed down as I felt a hitch in my side and a dribble of blood between my legs. I was wearing a palm fiber pad but it still was an unpleasant feeling.

"All right?" Ting asked.

"Yeah, just give me a second." I inhaled and exhaled as the pain subsided. "I'm fine. But keep talking."

"Three teachers. Who was your third?"

"A kponyungo."

She laughed hard. "Unusual!"

"Ssaiku is your only teacher?"

"Sorcerers typically only have one teacher, Najeeba, as a child is born of two parents."

I frowned.

"You will next go to Adoro 5?"

"Yes."

"We aren't far from there."

"I know."

"But you don't know when The Cleanser will come. It could come tomorrow, it could come in two years."

"I'll wait."

"And then?"

"I'll kill it."

"How?"

"I just will."

We were quiet again. Walking. I knew how I sounded. And I was bleeding. And I was starting to feel weak. But there was something else, and I didn't want to feel it. "I want to go lie down," I said, stopping.

Ting cocked her head. "It's okay."

"Then let's go." I walked toward the space between two tents. Somewhere, someone was laughing very hard and then there was the sound of plates breaking and more people started laughing.

"Najeeba," Ting called, but I walked faster. Doing so now hurt. I didn't care.

I felt a hand grasp my shoulder and pull me back.

"Don't touch me," I growled. Ting didn't let go, though. I was in too much pain now. I could feel blood running down my leg. I was wearing a loose dress, and I was glad there was no wind here to blow it against my ankles.

"It's all right," she said firmly.

I wouldn't look at her.

"Pride, even when warranted, can hold you back," she said.

I looked down, lifting a leg up. There was a small pool of blood. I laughed to myself. "I'm a mess."

"Messes can always be cleaned up," Ting said. "Najeeba, it's all right not to know what comes next."

I stared down at the growing pool of blood. Music came from the tent with the laughter. Someone had a guitar and someone had a talking drum. "I will kill it," I whispered.

"I don't doubt it. But you need to know how," she said. "I have an idea. But you have to get your pride out of the way."

I pressed my hands to my face hard enough to mash my nose. I loudly inhaled through my fingers, squeezing my eyes shut. Feeling the dull ache in my healing womb, the blood dribbling from between my legs, my sore leg, arm, shoulder, and back muscles, the mild dizziness. I slowly exhaled. I dropped my hands to my side and opened my eyes. "What is your idea?"

"We go to Adoro 5, as you already intended, and see what we can find in the Paper House," she said. "During an eclipse celebration, Ssaiku was very drunk. Over and over, he kept shouting, 'You can find anything at the library!' I asked him about it later and he said a library was an ancient Paper House." She stumbled around me, wildly kicking up her legs. "I can hear him yelling it right now, 'You can find anything at the library!!'"

Despite my mood, I couldn't help giggling. The image of Ssaiku being a loud and wild drunk was too much. I felt more blood seep out of me. "How far are we, do you think?"

"A day, maybe."

I groaned. My body still ached all over. It had only been a week. Walking still made me feel as if my insides would fall out. Could I do it? "Sssolu can't—"

"Your baby *and* Dedan will stay here." She touched my shoulder. "Ssolu will care for them both. You know this already."

I pressed my hands to my face and allowed myself. Just for a moment. I faced it. Ssolu would care for them if I went. The security of it. The way was clearing. My body ached and burned and leaked as I let all this wash over me. "Not yet," I said. "My body . . ."

Ting nodded. "You should heal some more first."

"A month," I blurted. It was a good idea. If we didn't go then, I'd never go. Motherhood, I'd missed it sorely and it was here again. My daughter. Dedan. Ssolu. Finally just stopping. There was the potential for family here. I even had a sort of "sister" in Ting, who was a woman who worked the Mystic Points and remembered The Before. Life and normalcy were calling me here.

However, I had something terrible to kill. And this would fulfill my father's wish. I needed to complete that story. I already knew the Paper House had one document about The Cleanser.

"Good," Ting said. "In a month, we will go. You and I. Your hard-headed daughter had a hard time listening. I'm glad you're different, at least in that way."

"Yes, Onyesonwu had a head like . . . stone," I said, shaking the blood from my ankle.

CHAPTER 4

Sssolu

For days, I did only three things, in no particular order: I ate pepper soup with chunks of chicken; I breastfed; I slept, Sssolu in my arms. I didn't even leave our tent. Now that I planned to leave in a month, I dedicated myself more strongly to healing. Dedan stayed sometimes and went at other times; I hadn't told him what Ting and I planned to do yet. Ting stopped by a few times. Ssaiku peeked in once, too. A few of the women came by, asking to take Sssolu. I'd been allowing them to take her so I could rest. I didn't let them, this time, though. They would have plenty of time with her when Ting and I went to Adoro 5.

Plus, I'd become wrapped in Sssolu's spell. She was a beautiful child, yes. She didn't cry much, easily the most present infant I'd ever seen. For being so young, this was uncanny. But it was so much more than that. Knowing that I was going to leave her for a bit, made me pull her closer to me. And when I did, I started gazing into her eyes as I cradled her. She'd gaze back. We'd stay like this for hours. Then she'd nurse, and while she did, I'd eat and we'd both sleep and then we'd go back to gazing at each other.

I saw things in her eyes. The first time was just after we'd both eaten and we were drowsy and content. I rested her on my legs, we locked eyes. "Ikuku," I whispered. "What do you dream about?"

She was on her back, looking down her tiny nose at me. As I looked at her, everything went a soft blue and the room grew hazy, as if the tent were filling with mist. I felt cool air waft in my face. And then, ever so gently, what I could only call tiny delicate stars of ice drifted around me. About four or five of them. I can say that they were ice because one landed on my leg, beside Sssolu. It was a pinprick of cold and melted quickly, like something that did not want to be there.

The stars of ice were the most substantial vision she gave me. However, in Sssolu's eyes, I also saw ethereal abstract things, geometric shapes, desert sky rainbows, mysterious lights. Once, I saw thousands of grey lines that moved together like a flock of birds. These various things were soothing at times, exciting at others, always they left me feeling in motion, as if I were traveling. I didn't know what any of it meant, and I don't think I was supposed to. You learn this lesson deeply when you become a sorcerer: You aren't always meant to know, and often you're simply meant to experience. During those close days with Sssolu, not even Dedan took her from me. Later, when he had his time with her, I wondered what she showed him and how. I suspected it was in a different way.

Near the end of the month, Ting came to see me. "Will you stay in here locked away with Sssolu until it's time to go?" she asked, laughing.

"Maybe," I muttered. It wasn't a terrible idea.

"How are you feeling?"

"My bleeding has mostly stopped, the pain . . ." I shrugged. "To be a woman is to know pain."

She nodded. "Let's take lunch outside."

"Okay. At the spot you took me to last time," I said. It was a quiet lonely place, a rare thing in the village of Ssolu. I liked it very much.

We brought a large pot of pepper soup (this soup was so delicious and it made my stomach feel better and somehow decreased my already dwindling pains), dates, cactus candy and a candy made from honey, and roasted goat meat. Ting also brought some weak palm wine and water. She pushed it on a small cart as I walked behind her, Sssolu strapped to my back with a piece of cloth. She cooed, and Ting said she was looking around "like she owns the place."

We didn't see many people on the way and I was glad. I suspect Ting took me this way for this reason. I didn't feel like chatting with anyone. I still felt as if I were in Sssolu's cocoon, and I didn't want to leave it just yet. Ting was welcome in it and Dedan, of course, but no one else. Not yet. The fresh air felt good and for the first time in over weeks, I yearned for open space. Real space. Outside the storm. The horizon. The direct sun, as opposed to the one that filtered through the brown of the storm or shined over its wall of wind, dust, and sand.

"Are you all right?" Ting asked.

"Yes," I said. "Some pain but manageable." My breasts were starting to fill up, but for now that didn't matter. Sssolu would take care of that when we settled down. What would I do about this when we left in a few days? Ah, that would be an experience.

We reached the outskirts and spread a blanket on the sand. The storm churned in the distance, and yet again I thought about the fact that I was living inside a great witch. I'd given birth inside one. Aro would smile and say this was as things should be. I unwrapped Sssolu and fed her. Just as she finished, Eyess came rushing up to us from between the nearest two tents.

"Ogasse Najeeba!" she shouted. "You're finally outside! I've been hoping and waiting! Is Ssssssssssolu with you?" All the children called her that when they were trying to be dramatic. And behind Eyess came five more children all around the same age of ten, two boys and three girls. All chanting Sssolu's name.

"We knew you'd come out soon. We've been hanging around here for days. Waiting and waiting!" Eyess announced. They danced around me and then crowded up to Sssolu.

I wanted to groan. Too many people. And loud children at that. Touching and poking and trying to grab my baby. Out of love. And maybe something else. I glanced at Ting, who was laughing. "Let it happen," she said.

That was the beginning of it. It was as if a signal went out to the village and everyone responded. Did they drop everything? Stop conversations? Grab friends and loved ones and siblings and parents and bring them along? Soon, there were women carrying Sssolu. There were men smoking and commenting on the day's dust formations at the top edge of the storm; apparently they looked like a bird in flight. Friends slapped the back of hands, surprised and happy to meet each other. Two parents of a child running with Eyess hugged each other, surprised to see each other here. Even the village chief Usson came and greeted me. I'd met him and the chieftess three days after I'd given birth, but I hadn't been very social then. Today, I wasn't much better. What was supposed to be a quiet lunch became a lively village gathering.

About a half hour into it all, I got up.

"No," Ting said, grabbing my arm. "Stay. You need this."

I narrowed my eyes at her and sat back down.

People brought more food. Chairs. Someone brought a guitar. A man began to sing as someone played it. Eyess and some of her friends danced in a circle chanting Sssolu's name. And throughout, Sssolu was greeted and passed around. I only saw her when I had to feed her again, and even then people talked to me as I did so. I changed Sssolu five times. Someone even brought me fresh baby clothes. Ting finally let me slip away hours later, near midnight, but only because Sssolu needed a bath.

My daughter drew the Vah together. Wherever she

went, they followed and they were happy. What a truly extraordinary thing. And so strikingly different from my beloved Onyesonwu, who seemed to have the opposite effect on the people of her community. As I walked back to our tent, I contemplated this and felt a sadness for my first daughter. She did such great things and she deserved so much better.

After twenty-five days, I was strong again. The pain was still there, that stretched and pummeled feeling lingering, but it was the type of pain you had when you knew you were nearly healed. The last few days, the women often came and took Sssolu, and I had been going for long silent walks with Ting. My aching muscles strengthened, my sore womb welcomed my body's movement, and my mind began to stretch now that Sssolu didn't have me so much in her grasp.

After our walk there, Ting had to go and see Ssaiku, and so there I was, alone in what had become my favorite spot (when not bothered with people) watching the storm. My breasts were filling with milk and the pressure was uncomfortable. I needed to find Sssolu soon. But for the moment, I was in the moment, watching the storm. Today, the dust formation on the top edge looked like a striding camel. I smiled to myself, thinking of Dedan who'd shown me a light purple sphere of glass he'd made using ash from a type of grass a child had brought him.

"It's a perfect circle," he'd said. "Look at it! I'll save it for Sssolu when she's old enough to appreciate it." He'd been so happy about having the time, the tools, and the skill to make it. And grateful. He kept repeating how grateful he was. Then he'd gone to find Sssolu so he could see if she liked touching it.

"Grateful," I said aloud, gazing at the storm. I sighed, feeling a tingle in my belly. I was on the brink and I didn't know it yet. I watched the storm a while longer, and then I went over the brink. Oh, it felt good and right to do so. I spoke it aloud, "I'm not going anywhere." Not yet. Not in a day or two. "Not ever," I whispered. It was as if a dust storm had been churning around me and my words and my choice quelled it. Everything that had been in motion stopped and fell. It was such a relief. My father had put me on a path to be a sorceress who would seek revenge for a great wrong. I *had* sought that revenge. But the fact was that at the end of that path was my death. Hadn't I seen it during my initiation? I'd come this far. And now, I would step *off* that path.

I exhaled as I admitted it to myself, again, as my

breasts filled with milk for my daughter. My father's desperate, terrified, grief-stricken request had been a sort of curse. Yes, I would step off that path.

I was home.

═══

That night, Ssaiku came for me at 3 AM. Dedan and I were asleep, and Sssolu was awake but content in my arms. Ssaiku walked right into our tent. "Najeeba," he said in his hard voice.

I sat up with Sssolu, instantly awake. "Ogasse?" I mumbled. Sssolu cooed. The Ssolu honorific for elders rolled right off my tongue. Again, I was reminded that I was home. "Is everything all right?"

Dedan was already on his feet.

"Dedan, take your daughter. Najeeba, come with me."

I handed Sssolu to Dedan. She snuggled against his bare chest. "What's happening?" he asked.

"Just talk, my friend, just talk," Ssaiku said.

I went out in my night dress, wrapping a blue veil over my bushy hair. It wasn't a cool night but it was windy, as usual. It felt good as we walked between the flapping tents. We stepped past the last of the tents on the village's opposite side of my favorite spot and we walked some more. Toward the storm. It was dark here, and Ssaiku didn't need to tell me to bring forth my kponyungo glow. I lifted from myself the slightest bit and blazed. We stopped when the wind stopped being the night's strong breeze and became the wind from the storm.

We stood there for a while. I felt powerful. I'd recently had life pass out of me a second time and now, here I stood. I relished the knowing and the fact that it was all over and done with. And now I would get to see Sssolu grow up. Dedan would be at my side. I was smiling to myself when Ssaiku finally spoke, "You will go the day after tomorrow."

I lost my glow, dropping back into my body. We were plunged into darkness. "I won't," I blurted. I looked toward him. I couldn't see his face. To speak to him in this way was a disrespect, I knew. I kept going. "Ogasse, I've decided. To go would be continuing a generational curse. I'm happy here. Sssolu is happy here. Dedan is happy here. This village is family. I see and understand it now."

"You'll finish what you started," he said.

I felt dizzy. I could feel my breasts leaking. The pain in my womb flared as it hadn't flared in a while.

I considered becoming the kponyungo and fleeing from him. "No," I shouted. "I don't have to! I can and I *will* make my own way!"

He said nothing.

I nodded. *Good,* I thought. *He understands.* The wind dried the tears of rage on my cheeks. But in that heavy darkness, the storm so close, its noise starting to gather weight, for the second time that day, I felt things falling around me. This time it was not because I'd decided to stop moving along what I knew was a path to my death, but because the idea of it was crumbling. I'd always believed I'd avenge my father. The need was in my bones. But for a little while, it was such a relief to believe I *could* make my own way.

I would have explored the Mystic Points, unlocked more of their secrets. I might have found a way back to my Onyesonwu. I would have gone to the wilderness again and spent time with the kponyungos; not years, but some time. I had loved it there far more than I would ever admit to anyone. Would Sssolu one day have been able to go with me? I'd have raised Sssolu with Dedan, surrounded and accompanied by a whole village. Dedan and I would have loved each other deeply. He'd have built a glass forest that he could deconstruct and rebuild each place Ssolu moved.

We'd have become Vah. Our skin would have been red-brown and their form of natural mysticism would have flowed through all three of us.

"It's not fair," I whispered.

"No. It's not."

"Do you know how it will end for you?"

He laughed. "Of course."

"Badly?"

"All death is terrible."

"I want so much I can never have."

"That is what makes you human, Najeeba."

"Ssaiku, how old are you?"

"That's not polite to ask."

I smiled. "You sound like a woman."

"Thank you."

"You won't tell me?"

"It doesn't matter. Will you go?"

I paused. "Yes."

"Good. Finish what you start. See it through. Your people need you."

"So does my daughter."

"Yes. She does." He paused and then said, "Najeeba, I had two sons. Twins. They would be older than you by now. Beautiful strange boys with muscles like gods, who could run faster than a falcon could fly, who laughed louder than ten men. They made this village so happy. No one ever asked for it, but one of them was going to be a sorcerer. You know that can happen?"

"I think—"

He continued, "Their mother Yinka was my best friend. She designed the most beautiful tents. Ssolu's tents were complex shapes. No wind could knock them down. It was as if they swallowed and digested the wind during storms. Everyone had a tent designed by her. When she passed, those tents were her legacy." He paused.

I was confused. The tents of Ssolu were sturdy, but they certainly were not complex.

"This was in The Before," he added.

I gasped, understanding. "No."

"My wife's legacy, her memory, and my sons . . ."

"Gone."

He looked pained. "No one remembers but Ting and me. They were taken out of the story. They are not in . . . the rewrite."

"Ogasse Ssaiku, I . . . oh Ani."

"While she was here, I kept my sons from Onyesonwu," he said. His voice was hard when he spoke her name. "I sensed she would bring pain. I just didn't know how. I thought I could manage her. My presence agitated her, Ting's did, too. Onyesonwu had not finished her training. She was like an open wound after a surgery. Unhealed. My caution wasn't enough. It could never have been enough." His hand suddenly lit a bright red, and he held it up. The entire area glowed a harsh red. His face was hard, angry. I stepped back. "It is *not* fair," he said. He pointed at me and his words were a snarl. "But you *finish* what you *start*."

We held each other's eyes in the red light. I could smell the milk leaking from my breasts. His wrinkles were so deep that I imagined grains of sand hiding in the folds. He was always so serious, I doubted he would care. "You don't have to tell me again," I said. I wanted to get away from him, but I also wanted to prove to him that Onyesonwu hadn't taken from him out of spite. We were noble women who righted wrongs. If we did harm, that harm was a page in a book of good.

He left me alone there in the dark.

CHAPTER 5

The Type of Women We Are

In the morning, I was introduced to someone interesting. I'd only heard of them in stories. Someone's sister's best friend's brother would spot one from afar running fast. Or there would be rumor of a herd of them living somewhere too far to personally check. An elder would find strange footprints in the mud after it rained. They were characters in old stories told by mothers. They were drawings made by children.

"His name is Aejej," Ting said as she led me through the camel corral.

"Why does the corral have to be in the middle of the village? I'd have thought it would be on the outside, so they could have more space."

"They don't like the noise of the storm."

We stopped at one of the thatch huts where some of the camels liked to sleep. In front of the entrance was a large ball made of raffia. "Aejej likes to play with that," Ting said, kicking it aside. We stepped up to the entrance. I gasped. He was more beautiful than I expected and nothing like the drawings of children. His coat was a reddish brown, darker than Tende's. His feet and head and mane were a glossy black, like wings of a darkling beetle.

"How?" I whispered as Ting stepped into the hut. The horse nickered softly and nudged her as she caressed his snout.

"Aejej came to us," she said. Her words reminded me of Tende, who'd come to Luyu. "I bring the storm down once a month for a day. Gives everyone a chance to go to town, enjoy the silence, stretch, see the distance, watch the sunset. We all need it. Well, this time, hours after I brought the storm back up, come night when I went to look over the camels, we found we had a new and . . . different 'camel.' He may have been driven out of his clan, he may have left it, I do not know. He was competing with two other camels to lick the salt block."

"Can you . . . ride him?" I asked.

She laughed. "Only me." She paused. "I convinced him with nsibidi."

I laughed. "How?"

"Nsibidi is convincing," she said, leading Aejej out. I stepped back. He was so magnificent, but a power exuded from him that was more intimidating than a bigger camel. Oh, my mother would have loved this animal. Me? I was afraid of him.

"Relax," Ting laughed. "If he senses your fear, that's all he needs."

I took a deep breath and stilled myself.

"You really want to leave tomorrow?" she asked.

For the first time since she'd shown me the horse, my attention left it. "Yes."

"Don't let Ssaiku pressure you," she said.

"He is not."

"He feels great resentment toward your daughter."

"I'm aware." I held a hand out for Aejej to sniff. The horse sniffed it, and I easily held my ground as he stepped closer to me. "Even people who hate you can be right about you."

"Ssaiku doesn't hate you."

A part of him did. "We leave tomorrow," I said. What I didn't say was that Ssaiku's words stung me deeply. I'd wanted to step off my path, a selfish, cowardly thing. I knew it was my own fear of death. I was supposed to be my daughter's mother. I was the woman who had given her a name that defiantly asked, "Who

Fears Death?" And when I stepped off my path, even for that short time, I'd felt so light, so happy, so relieved, I felt so much hope. I saw a beautiful future. I was supposed to be my daughter's mother.

Then Ssaiku had come and slapped me awake. He'd talked about duty and sacrifice without talking about it. The memory of his sons and wife all gone. More casualties of my daughter's actions that saved the world. Who was I to turn from a duty that would save my people? Who was I to choose not to sacrifice? Just so that I could have a beautiful future? Who was I? I knew who I was. My name meant, "She who knows." It is not only about knowing. It is what you do with the knowing.

A name is one's destiny. Always.

═══

Dedan paced around huffing and puffing. He paused, looked at me and then he shook his head like an agitated camel. Then he continued pacing. His energy reminded me of the day he destroyed the glass house. There was no stopping wherever his mind was going. This time, I waited for him to land. After five minutes, he stopped and glared at me again. His eyes watered and his nostrils flared.

He whirled around, wiped his face with his hand and pointed a finger at me, his eyes narrowed, "Do *not* let that thing kill you."

His eyes were so wild that it took me a moment to respond. "What?" I asked. "W-why do you—?"

"For nearly nine months I've been trying to figure out how to keep you from getting yourself killed," he blurted. We were in our small tent and he spoke quietly. The Vah lived close to each other, and it was not an easy place for privacy. The tents were luxurious, but a tent was a tent, which meant their "walls" were thin. He stepped close to me. "I always felt that as long as you carried our baby, I could keep you close . . . somewhat." He paused, narrowing his eyes at me. He was hinting at my journeys as the kponyungo. "But now that Sssolu is here, that has changed. I have always accepted you as what you are, always. But I won't—"

"Stop. I'm not confronting The Cleanser yet," I snapped. "I'm just going to the Paper House, finding that piece of paper that tells about it and coming back."

"You say that. But you also do what you do when you do it," he said.

I paused at this. He was right.

"If that thing appears while you are in Adoro 5, it will kill you," he said, throwing up his hands.

"You think so?"

"Yes." We glared at each other. He knew everything about me. He knew how much I had mastered, what I'd studied, suffered, and grown from, and he thought The Cleanser would kill me. So easily. "There is so much at work here," he said. "You know this but you have this tunnel vision when you decide something. It's your strength and your weakness, Najeeba. Listen to me, now, though, please." He was grasping my shoulders, breathing hard.

Sssolu was somewhere with some women, and I was glad. There was a reason her name was not part of this conversation. The village would care for her if I went. Both Dedan and I knew this. Sssolu would be fine. Dedan would be fine. "If that thing came for you right now, I would kill it for you," Dedan said, wrapping his arms around me. I rested my head on his shoulder. My breasts ached. I needed to find Sssolu to feed her.

═══

We left in the early morning. Ting had an old portable that she used for its GPS capabilities, but also its music. She played a soft guitar tune that made me a little sad. I hadn't been able to say goodbye to Sssolu because she'd spent the night with a group of women. But I made sure to express and save a whole jar of milk for her. From this point on, I'd have to express and discard my milk as we travelled to keep it flowing. Dedan had gone out before I woke up. To go where, I didn't know. He'd left a tiny blue prism on our mat, and as Ting and I rode, I held it in the sunshine. It separated the light into various shades of blue.

MorningStar had refused when I went to get her that morning. It was not a long trip, only about a day. She could do that easily. When I approached her, she'd been happy to see me, sniffing and nudging me. She'd nuzzled at my belly, and I told her that Dedan and Sssolu were well. I fed her dates, which she greedily lapped up. She was herself . . . except she wouldn't get up to leave with me.

She refused to move. When I tried to pull her reign harder, she'd stood up and roared at me. I stumbled back, confused. "What?" I asked. But she simply sat back down and scowled at me. I've known many camels. I know what one who has made up her mind looks like. MorningStar was known for firmly making up her mind. She turned away when she saw my tears and did not follow me when I went to Tende, who stood up right away. And just like that, the choice was made. Tende and Aejej would take Ting and me to Adoro 5.

When we introduced them, Tende and Aejej didn't like each other. Tende had even taken a nip at Aejej, and Aejej had pinned his ears back, snuffed and run off, stopping dangerously close to where the storm's winds began to pick up. Ting had been annoyed but not very worried. "He does that often," she said. "His flight instinct is strong. He will come back to me." And he had.

We stopped at the edge of the village. Watching Ting pull down the storm was something I wouldn't forget. Before us, the storm churned. We'd left the camel and horseback near the village edge and walked as close to the storm as we could without being lashed by its dust and sand. The storm was so powerful that I could feel the ground vibrating. The howl made speaking useless. It felt like being in the presence of a masquerade, and I wouldn't have had the arrogance to speak even if I wanted to.

She raised her hands and in the air she drew nsibidi symbols that only she could see. But there was also something she was doing deep in her throat, a low humming that I felt vibrating in the back part of my head. The sound she made somehow scaled even the noise of the storm.

Suddenly everything fell away. I was suspended in a void, even as I saw everything around me. Ting held up a hand to the storm and spread her long fingers, her palm facing the storm. She opened her mouth. Maybe she inhaled, I couldn't tell, I couldn't hear. I was floating and trying to understand why, because I looked like I was just standing beside her.

Then the storm . . . stopped. It was like a swiftly spinning wheel grabbed by someone very strong. Ting motioned her hands, pulling something down. The sand and dust began to fall, the sound soft and heavy at the same time. A cloud of dust bloomed and rolled over and beyond us, but I could breathe just fine. Ting was protecting us and the village. The feeling of being suspended in emptiness went away. It was replaced by a heavy muted silence.

"Is it difficult to do?" I asked. My voice sounded clear, every part of its pitch crisp.

"Yes," she said. Her eyes were narrow and she was holding herself gingerly. She looked about to vomit. After a moment, she said, "But I do it so often. I'm used to it. It feels like . . . something stopping my heart." She didn't *look* used to it. "No powerful juju is without consequence," she added. I patted and grasped her shoulder. Her eye twitched.

"You're still a human being," I said.

She looked away. I hadn't let go of her shoulder. "I am the one who brings it down and lifts it up."

"Every time?"

She nodded.

"What of Ssaiku?"

"He's old. And it's not his job."

"You're still human."

"So are you."

We looked into each other's eyes, regarding the pain and loneliness within each other. It is a thing to be the type of women we are. Ting broke the gaze first, moving from my grasp. "I know how to care for myself," she said.

I nodded. "Good."

"Do you?"

I laughed. "Not really."

"Dedan is good for you. Sssolu is good for everyone."

We walked with Tende and Aejej for about two miles and then she turned and lifted the storm back up. We rested for an hour, she slept, and I expressed as much milk as I could and slept a bit. And then we started toward Adoro 5.

CHAPTER 6

White is Not for Bleeding

Ting traded a small sack of ceede, beautiful red gemstones, at the shop near the Paper House that specifically sold white and modest women's clothing. I felt strange wearing white, especially since all the walking and camel riding had made me start bleeding again. Not a lot of blood, but enough to ruin a white dress. But the Paper House had rules. I used a few layers of cloth in my undergarments and hoped it was enough.

My dress was light, reaching my ankles, managing to gather the dust that puffed as I walked. The dress fit my tall body, gently hugging my hips and loose enough to give my enlarged breasts room to move freely. There was a warm soft breeze and as the dress fluttered, it reminded me of the periwinkle garments I wore when I walked in human spirit form. I felt good in this dress, very much like myself.

Ting, on the other hand, wasn't aching from giving birth a little over a month ago and leaking from breast-feeding, yet she was even more uncomfortable. She'd chosen to buy loose pants and a white kaftan that fit her body snuggly; it looked like something styled in Banza. On top of this, she was Vah, of the Red People, a people who covered their skin with red palm oil.

"Let it stain," I said with a shrug. I was now in the habit of rubbing the palm oil into my skin, too, but it was the least of my problems. "You won't see it until you take the clothes off anyway."

She nodded. "This is a one-time thing. I will throw these clothes away when we leave."

She tugged at her clothing as we walked to Tende and Aejej. "It feels like something made for a man. Why is it crushing my breasts like this? And these pants feel like they are trying to crawl inside my crotch."

I laughed, stuffing our folded up clothes in Aejej's pack. "This is why I prefer dresses."

"Only Ssolu clothes can make me happy," she mumbled. "And white is silly to wear."

"That, I very much agree with." I'd never thought much of it, but white wasn't a good color to demand of girls and women who often had to deal with blood.

We led Tende and Aejej to a camel pen, paying the

camel keeper some ceede to water and feed them. She was about seventeen years old and she'd grinned with delight when she saw Tende and Aejej. "They're so beautiful," she breathed. "Is it all right if I bring my friends and we brush them?"

"Of course," Ting said, laughing. "Thank you."

"What are their names?" the girl asked, excitedly.

"Tende is the camel, the horse is Aejej," Ting said.

"They're like juju animals from a story!" the girl said. She looked beyond us, put her two fingers between her lips and whistled loudly. Three other girls who'd been nearby selling groundnuts were rushing over as Ting and I walked away.

"They'll probably smell like scented oil when we come back," I said, holding my dress as a gust of wind blew it against my hips.

Ting was unbothered. "Tende and Aejej are used to being treated like royalty."

I linked my arm in hers, and we walked down the road I'd walked down so many times. Since we'd entered Adoro 5, I hadn't let myself take it in. Not fully. We'd entered town on the east side, the opposite side of where I'd lived. I felt like weeping. Everything looked the same, but it was not the same. The people were mostly Okeke, but there were a few Nuru. The homes were a little bigger and many of the ones I knew were still where I'd last seen them. We passed my friend Obi's house. My agemate, then boyfriend and later lover, Obi had gotten married and never spoken to me again. I couldn't remember if he'd moved away or not. The house he'd lived in was about twice the size it had been. Had the very land that Adoro 5 rested on expanded in The Now? I locked down my emotions, channeling the kponyungo to distance myself.

As I walked toward the Paper House, my arm linked with Ting's, I let them wash over me. My hometown no longer existed. I could never go back. I felt the breath of it, and I grasped Ting's arm more tightly, feeling lightheaded with understanding. The finality of it was heavy, and I felt alone. Yes, I had Dedan and Sssolu, Tende and Aejej. Aro, Sola, and the kponyungo Sonnn I'd spent the equivalent of years with in the wilderness. Even Ting and the Vah. I had people. But my father, mother, brothers, my daughter Onyesonwu, they were all gone. Everyone now in my life was new.

"You all right?" Ting asked.

I nodded.

"Focus on what's ahead," she said, motioning toward what was literally ahead.

CHAPTER 7

The Paper House

The Paper House had changed. A lot. I grinned as we stood before it. I grinned because I knew this change was not a product of The Now, it was because of my *family*. Because of *me*. Because of the wealth I had earned Adoro 5. The Paper House that had been ravaged by the Nuru long ago in The Before was now the size of *three* houses. Those walking in and coming out were Okeke women but there were also more than a few Nuru women and in several cases, they were entering *together*. All were wearing the traditional and required white garments one wore in the Paper House.

The front doors were still a vibrant blue that glowed brightly in the sunshine. And the wrought iron handles still said "bass vah," which I'd since learned meant "to throw a sign" in the dead language of Vah.

"The language of Vah has nothing to do with my people," Ting said when I showed it to her. "It is only a linguistic coincidence."

"Like Okike Mystic Point and Okeke people?" I asked.

"Indeed. It happens."

The doors were still heavy, only budging when you put strength into it. You nearly had to get angry to get it to move. Today that wasn't difficult for me. "Move," I muttered giving it a great shove.

Ting chuckled. "This place has so many requirements," she said. "I like it."

"Get ready for the disinfecting mist," I said. "It'll feel like the cold from a capture station."

The blast of cold air wafted over us. It smelled earthy and familiar.

"Is it laced with perfumed oil, too?" Ting asked.

"I don't know," I said. "That could just be the spirit of the Paper House."

We stepped into a very different Paper House than the one I'd grown up visiting. Oh yes, it was still full of women reading tomes and papers. The walls were still blue. There were still wooden desks and dusty stone floors. But the place was no longer a large one-story house with rows and rows and aisles and aisles and stacks and stacks of neatly arranged books, pamphlets, and documents. It was three stories high and twice as wide.

For a moment, we stood there, taking it all in. It was then that I noticed there were not only women in here, there were men, too. Everyone was here, albeit, still mostly various women.

"How does one navigate this place?" Ting asked.

I laughed. "You don't. You let it lead you."

"We don't have time for that."

I nodded. "We need to find the overseer."

But first, we walked around a bit.

"This is the largest Paper House I've ever seen," Ting said.

"How many have you been to?"

"Five," she said. We stopped at a wall stacked with dusty crumbling papers. There were no labels, words, or symbols on them. The Paper House didn't classify things with specificity, though there was order. We needed the overseer. He was the only one who knew the order of things in the Paper House.

Ting gently pulled out a piece of paper that was sitting at the top of a stack near the wall. It was thick, yellowed, coiled, and small. She looked at it.

"What is it?" I asked.

"A recipe for soup," she said, putting it back. "It uses camel meat. I do not eat camel meat."

We strolled about the large space, watching people. They sat at desks reading, stood in corners discussing, some riffled through stacks and stacks of papers, piles of books. Everyone seemed mostly content and occupied, except for a woman sitting on the dusty floor surrounded by books, weeping as she looked and threw a book aside. No one bothered her, she was only bothered by whatever she was doing and thinking.

Incense burned in corners, the air was cool, and there was a general sense of curiosity. I remembered clearly why I loved this place. I'd never been a big reader but the sense of great knowledge living here made me never want to leave. However, we were here for a specific reason and that sense of urgency tamed any compulsion I had to amble and aimlessly explore.

The overseer's tiny office space was in the center of the Paper House, where it had always been. It almost seemed like the building had grown around it. You had to move through a maze of shelves and stacked documents. These were probably the oldest stacks in the Paper House, the first items to be collected. The air here smelled of old books, oils, herbs, ink, and dust. From what I recalled, the overseer only spent the night here. It was rare for him to be anywhere but looking over shoulders, correcting, showing and chastising patrons, restocking, shelving, and protecting books and papers. But today, here he was. Sitting on a couch made of black and white goat skin and eating . . . a bowl of soup. I glanced at Ting and knew she was wondering the same thing—did it have camel meat in it?

"Overseer," I said. "I'm sorry to disturb your meal."

He was very old now, being about the age my father would have been. He was still tall and gangly with strong hands and well-kept nails. And he still had those clear eyes that seemed to look deep into you and easily locate that which you were seeking, whether you knew it or not. His white garments didn't have a spot on them. I never understood how he did this. He cocked his head and squinted at me. "You. The one who likes the dangerous books."

I laughed, surprised. "You remember me?"

"I don't remember many. Curious girls who read are common, but the ones who find and nearly die from reading dangerous books are rare . . . and memorable."

"It's good to see you," I said.

"Where have you been?"

"Away."

He narrowed his eyes at me. "You look the same. Who is this Red woman?"

"I am Ting," she said. "I'm a sorceress of Ssolu."

"Ssolu? You must hate wearing the white."

"Very much."

"I appreciate your respect. Thank you for coming, sorceress. The Paper House is honored. Ah, I see now. You're here to learn more about the Mystic Points."

Before Ting could respond, I said, "I'm also a sorceress now . . . a sorcerer."

He laughed. "No surprise there."

"The Mystic Points are not why we're here, though. I need to find information about something I want to kill."

"Oh?"

I wasn't sure if I should speak it. Most Osu-nu in all the various Adoro villages saw The Cleanser as a necessary and assumed thing. They did not question its existence. They revered those who were taken when they returned because those who The Cleanser took were always beautiful, they attracted a natural respect, they were highly sought after. The way my father spoke of his older sister had been as if she were a secret queen. Those taken and returned by The Cleanser when

I was growing up were always the most popular, had the most marriage prospects, were given the greatest business opportunities, had the most everything. I never questioned any of it. Not until that day I saw it with my kponyungo eyes for what it was. That tall figure in dirty garments, was *not* a man. It was a monster.

"So . . . you remember me because of that day, right?" I suddenly asked.

"How do you remember . . . that day?" he asked. "Do you recall the books that were here? What they were about?"

"Yes," I said.

He frowned. ". . . What about how this place was attacked?!"

I froze. "*You* remember The Before?"

His eyes began filling with tears. His voice was small when he spoke, "Is that what you call it?"

"Yes."

"Oh Ani," he breathed, pressing his large hands to his face and was like that for a long moment. I sat down on the couch beside him and put my hand on his back. Ting and I waited. When he brought his hands down, tears still poured from his eyes and his brow was deeply furrowed. "*No one* else remembers," he whispered. "I don't believe I am mentally broken. I know myself. I am the overseer and have been since I was a young man. I guard knowledge here in the Paper House, but also here in the mind." He tapped his forehead. "I'm an elder now and that has not changed. But, oh Ani, to know of a different world, a different *time* when not one person around you knows of it, to see many of the books here, and papers, even the dangerous ones, to see them *shift* . . ." He gasped, more tears falling from his eyes.

"I was walking down a corridor when this building shook. When it shifted and changed shape. The wealth you brought back then allowed us to expand on this place after that Nuru attack. Still, I saw two more rooms grow right before my eyes. It was like the Paper House was alive and living but an impossible type of alive because no known animal or plant can grow a large part of its body within seconds." He shook his head, as if trying to shake the memory away. "The book in my hands went from being a book about vultures to one about owls! When I stepped outside, all of Adoro 5 was different; some people were different, some people were gone, some seemed to appear. See all the Nuru and they are kind people, like the hate never happened! It is beautiful, but when you remember, it's strange, confusing, there's a feeling that some of the ugliness is still there, like blood stains that remain after a crime has been cleaned up. Ah, I've felt like something left behind. I have had to carry this. I am quiet about it. Otherwise people would think I'm mad. For a while, I wondered if I was!"

He wept some more. The overseer. A tough, scary and strong man whom I didn't know well, but who had been close friends with my father. When he calmed, he asked me again, "What is it that you need to kill?"

"The Cleanser."

More tears came to his eyes now, but he did not look distraught. He was smiling, ruefully, and he was clenching his fists. "The world is fixing itself."

Ting and I looked at each other. A shiver travelled up my spine.

"It is evil," he whispered. He glanced behind him, toward his office entrance.

"How do you know?" Ting asked.

"Because I'm the overseer. I have access to a lot of information. The document you seek, I have seen it and it was not destroyed during the attack nor was it . . . changed. And I know exactly where it is. It was one of the first things I read when I was initiated into the secret society to be overseer. It is . . . one of the dangerous documents."

"Can you take us to it?"

"First . . . where have you come from?" he asked. He glanced at Ting and spoke before I could answer. "The desert?"

We both nodded.

"Nuru women and men, I see them plenty now. But it's rare to see one of the Vah here."

"We have little reason to leave the desert," she said. "Usually the desert holds all the answers we seek."

"Understood. The desert holds all of Earth's many layers," he said. "Compounded memories of survival, of creation, of death. Always an ocean, even without the water."

Ting smiled, nodding. The overseer smiled, too, as if they both shared an intimate joke. He patted her on the shoulder.

The overseer led us out of his office to the other side of the Paper House. Here the hallway grew narrow into a stack aisle, books stacked on both sides of us. Then it grew dark as he led us downward. There were no stairs, but you could see the gradual decline. Eventually, it was clear that we were underground. It was cooler, the air smelled dank and moist and there was a compressed stillness. We passed no one and, if we had, it would have been a tight squeeze.

When we arrived at an iron gate blocking our passage, we stopped. It looked like something my beloved husband Fadil would have constructed. It was heavy, but every inch of it was shaped. The edges were scalloped and rounded, there were nsibidi signs all over it. I had a feeling it hadn't changed at all during the move to The Now.

"No one is allowed here, but me," he said.

Ting stepped up to the gate and ran a finger over the symbols. "Who made this?!" she asked. "This is . . ." her eyes were wide with wonder. She turned back to the symbols. "So expertly written."

"I don't know who made it," he said. "The dangerous books and papers have always been kept here. That circular journal you found when you were a teen, Najeeba, the one that would have pushed and stranded your mind in a distant place if you'd kept reading the thing, it got out. Escaped. It can be that way with a lot of these dangerous manuscripts. They are like a herd of goats—if you don't constantly herd them together, they will all keep scattering their separate ways. Dangerous documents will seek to return to their preferred place, just as domesticated goats will always fight domestication. I spend much of my time finding and bringing dangerous documents back to their special room. That journal you read was about traveling, so it moves around more than the others."

It had been written by a woman who could . . . move about, and it had helped me understand my own ways of witching.

"Go ahead," Ting said. "I want to stay here and look at this gate."

The overseer and I went on.

"It's not much further," he said.

Still, by the time we stopped, minutes later, he was lighting the way with his portable. The way was so narrow that we had to move sideways. The ceiling was so low that it nearly touched my head. And above were woven slots that housed books or papers.

"I've always wondered, how do you keep track of everything, overseer?"

He tapped his head. "It's all in here. You are a sorceress—"

"I'm a sorcerer," I corrected.

"Sorcerer, sorry. To be one, you are moving with certain natural skills. It is similar to being an overseer. You have to have the natural ability to contain it all. Then you learn skills to enhance it." He stopped and turned to me. "Since I was about three years old, I have been able to remember every detail of my life, everyone I have met, all that I have seen. To be overseer, you have to have this type of skill. Now, imagine how it is for me with this Before and Now? I contain it all and no one, until you two, remembers it."

"There are others who remember," I said. "I'm sorry you've been so alone here."

He continued on. "I'm always alone, anyway. But at least I know I haven't gone mad or been cursed."

"You're not mad, but I don't know about the curse part."

The narrow way opened into a small round space with a ceiling and walls and floor made of smooth stone. There were few books here, all of them stacked neatly in wooden shelves on the far side of the space. I tapped at the shiny floor with my sandal.

"The oldest part of the Paper House. Someone carved this room from the giant stone they found here," he said. "We'll never know how. I sometimes wonder if it was used before there even was a Paper House."

"How far underground are we?"

"Only about twenty feet." He went to the closest shelf. He brought a pair of black goat fur gloves from his pocket. "Hopefully it's here."

"When I found it, it was on a stack of documents near the front."

He chuckled and said, "I suspect if you or your friend stay in the Paper House much longer, you'll leave me with a lot of searching and reshelving to do." He shook his head. "Yes, they're like goats."

He looked at the shelf and moved to the side where stacks of papers were squeezed into the end of the shelf. He squatted before it and removed the upper part of the stack. I stood behind him.

"Can I help?" I asked.

"Absolutely not," he said. "There are things in here that are itching for a sorcerer's touch to awaken them."

"I can control—"

"No need to take that risk," he snapped. "Step back."

He picked up a paper and placed it into the new stack. "It's in here, I think." He held up a small yellow booklet. "This is full of laughter and poison." He put it on the new stack. He held up a piece of black paper. "I don't know what this is, but if you hold it for too long, you begin to smell smoke." He held up a booklet. "Each of these documents is what I call a manifester– they bring forth things. It's why they are best kept here, all together, bound tightly to muffle their intent as much as I can. I am no sorcerer—"

"But you have our ways," I said.

"To remember every second of one's life, to use that ability in a Paper House, that kindles some things," he said. He paused and held up a piece of paper. "Ah. Here it is." He gingerly picked it up, gently holding it between his gloved fingertips. The flimsy circular piece of paper was grey with dirt, creased and stained with darker splotches that might have been blood. The irony wasn't lost on me that the only thing in all of Adoro 5 about The Cleanser was all on a single round piece of dirty paper.

My belly flipped. The piece of paper was smaller than I remembered it. Barely the size of my hand. He held it out to me. I didn't move. This was a big part of what I'd come all this way for. There were answers on that paper. Answers that I could probably understand now.

The way he was carrying it made me think about that woman's journal that I had picked up with my naked hands back when I was a teen, unaware that it was a volatile object. Aro had a few similar objects in his hut. They were objects soaked with juju or a natural mysticism that required you to handle them with care. I'd once picked up a small clay pot, and he'd found me sitting on the floor of his hut hours later, saliva dribbling from the corner of my mouth. He'd had to dump a bucket of water on me to bring me back, and even then there was a tiny tornado of dust swirling in a corner for weeks afterward.

I took the piece of paper with my bare hand. "Ugh," I said, nearly dropping it. It was rough and scratchy and, immediately, an image flashed through my mind of a large black venomous spider perched on the inside of my hand. I twitched, but held the paper firmly. "When something is aware of you make sure it knows you are not a coward," Aro had once told me.

This paper was very aware of me, and it didn't want me to know its information. No, not the paper, the knowledge. Knowledge can have an awareness, I realized. Up to now, I'd only encountered knowledge that wanted to be known. I let out a breath. I could see the spider now, clinging to my hand, a sharp leg poking through the paper.

I don't like spiders. I never have. I'd been bitten by a large one once while on the salt roads. I'd been sleeping on my mat when I felt the sting. The bite had not been so terrible, it was the way it had clung to me as it dug its fangs in. I'd barely been able to slap it off. It had then slipped so smoothly into the dark that neither I nor my brothers and father could find it. Evil thing.

"You've lost," I said now to the knowledge living in the paper. And gradually, the spider let go and crept back in. When I flipped it over, it was gone. I shuddered.

"What did you see?" the overseer asked.

"It doesn't matter," I said. I held the paper close to my eyes. Now it was soft. Old. Thin. Flimsy. But it would not crumble to dust any time soon. Every letter was perfect and the same style as the other letters of its kind. Every number, too. As if it had been done by a spirit.

"It was written by a machine," he said. "Printed."

"Play for The Cleanser," it said at the top. The rest was written in such tiny print that I had to squint. "We youths will break it. We will destroy it. For our elders and our ancestors, because they cannot. For Ngozika Ogbu. Because though wounded, she tried, and then she died. We are the help she never received. We will finish what she started. Remember, master and then play and get the answer. With this, we end it."

The rest was so tiny that reading it made my head throb. If I held it far from me, the symbols looked like a square shadow. With the stains and dirt, it was even harder to read. It was nsibidi that was too complex for me to decipher. I had learned some of this mystical language, but I was no master of it. Had it, too, been written by machine? Maybe Ting could decipher it.

Frustrated, I held it close to my face. What was The Cleanser? How could I kill it? Those were what I needed to understand. I needed to know *something*. Now. I managed to interpret some of it closer to the center of the paper: "Spirit from the wilderness. Thief of impactful destiny. It will replace what it takes with worthless treasure. It is the Great Liar."

I felt dizzy. The world around me swam and I stumbled.

"Stop reading," the overseer said, grasping my shoulder. "It's beginning to take from you."

He was right. I could feel it drawing my strength right through my hands. They felt warm and red, the tips touching the paper cool. But I *needed* to know it all. I pushed to read more.

Citizens of a Strange Class . . .

Everything went black.

═══

I was looking into Ting's face. "That was stupid," she said, taking her hand from my cheek. She blew on it and rubbed her hands together. I groaned, my forehead throbbing. Immediately, I remembered all that I'd read. I wanted to become the kponyungo, fly to a quiet part of the desert and think about it.

"Najeeba, focus," Ting said. "We are in the heart of the Paper House. You've found what you needed."

I shook my head. I understood what she was saying, but the urge to leave was so strong.

"Is she all right?" the overseer asked.

"I feel like I should slap her," Ting said, frowning. Instead, she pulled me up. "Najeeba, come on!"

With her help, I struggled to my feet. I was still grasping the paper. Ting plucked it from my hand. She looked at it and grimaced and then brought a handkerchief from her pocket. She spat into it. Then she looked at the paper with disgust. "Vile thing," she said.

I was feeling better already. "It's awful."

"Take this," the overseer said, holding out a piece of goat fur.

Ting took it and put the paper in the fur. "Thank you."

"Goat fur protects against a lot of these dangerous documents," he said. "I don't know why."

"My teacher Ssaiku says goats consume harmful and old juju," Ting said. "It never kills or even harms them. He thinks there's something they are born with."

Holding it with the goat fur, she opened up the paper and looked at it. I looked, too, and immediately began to feel woozy. I stepped back.

"It has a smell," Ting said. "Like blood."

"Can you read it?" I asked, swallowing hard. I was nauseous and, for a moment, I was sure that I would vomit. Instead I belched and immediately felt better. I stepped further away.

"Yes," she said. "But it's uncomfortable."

I nodded. "The nsibidi?"

"Yes. But not here." She looked at the overseer.

He frowned. "It is against my rules."

"Rules are meant to sometimes be broken," Ting insisted.

I braced myself. She didn't know the overseer.

"I've been gracious enough to bring you down here and show you these things," he said.

"We're appreciative," Ting said. "And asking you to be even more gracious."

"I have never allowed anyone to take anything from the Paper House," he said firmly. "The only time in my decades as overseer anyone has taken *anything* from here was when those Nuru attacked. They nearly killed me in order to do so. I fought three of them off and another five came and beat me. One of them smashed my arm using a book of maps. When every thing changed again, that was the only thing that changed about me, my arm is no longer difficult." He was breathing heavily now, his eyes wet with tears. "I fought them when they tried to take from here. I wouldn't allow it. I guard the documents in this place. From everything."

"Overseer, I want to *kill* The Cleanser," I hissed. "The Paper House is the home of knowledge. It's one of the souls of our people. The Cleanser takes destiny. Another of our people's souls! That is what that paper says. How to end a soul killer is here in the Paper House, on this piece of paper. That is no coincidence. You have protected it. That is no coincidence. *Sometimes rules are meant to be broken*! You have to be the one to break it."

He scowled at me, more tears falling from his eyes. His nostrils flared, his breathing heavy.

"Things are better now," I said. "They did not change on their own. Someone had to step up and sacrifice to make it happen, and now so many are better off. You remember. But there are still things that need to be fixed. And again, it is up to someone. You are one of them now, as I am."

He pounded his fist against his thigh. He said nothing as Ting brought a raffia sack from her pocket. She put the paper enveloped in goat fur in the sack. She cinched it shut with its drawstring and held it out to me. I took it and looked at the overseer, but he wouldn't look at me. He turned his back.

We left him that way, finding our way out on our own. It took us an hour. And as we stepped into the sunlight and walked down the street past the shop selling white clothing, only then did I look back. He was not standing in any of the windows, and I could not see into the Paper House doors. I knew I could never return there again. That way was shut to me. I would never see the overseer again. Another door to my past was closed.

"The roads are a little different," I said.

We were walking to my parents' house and I was finding it a little confusing. Things were mostly the same, but there were twists and turns on the dirt roads and a few homes in different places that made getting there take a bit longer. It was pleasantly cloudy and after the dank darkness of the lower level of the Paper House, it was nice to be outside.

"You can still find it, though?" Ting asked.

"Yes," I said. And we did. There was now a hill beside the house and, at its top, I stopped and sat down, my back against a dead palm tree. Ting sat beside me. There was the stable where my camel Abdul, mama's camel Noor, and papa's camel Dusty stayed. In the back, I could see a hint of what used to be my mother's garden, which I used to maintain. It still looked lush. I even thought I saw a hint of cactus candy growing. "I wonder . . . who's living there," I said. "Maybe my brother's children or . . ." I didn't want to say it, and I didn't want to see it. I couldn't bear the thought of strangers living there.

Two young women walked up to the house holding hands. One had black braids that were so long they reached the ground, their tips collecting sand like those of a priestess. The other wore the periwinkle garments of a woman who has come from Holding Conversation with the annual group of women in the desert. The two were discussing something and they did not stop talking as they entered the house.

"Do you know them?" Ting asked.

I shook my head. Could they have been my nieces? I would not have recognized them. If they were strangers, I didn't feel upset about it and that was good. "Let's go," I said.

Aejej and Tende indeed did smell of perfumed oil, Aejej's mane was a series of braids and both of their coats were glossy and soft. They were surrounded by girls when we came back to the corral and saying goodbye took nearly twenty minutes.

"You've eaten well," I said to Tende as we made

our way up the road. "But I'll bet you're glad to get away." Aejej was already far ahead, moving at a trot. The moment we were outside of Adoro 5, Ting dismounted him, and removed his saddles and reigns.

"What are you doing?" I asked, dismounting. "Why take a break here?"

When Aejej immediately began to roll around in the dust, I understood. When I did the same to Tende, he rolled, too. Neither animal liked smelling of perfume and though the brushing was nice, they didn't like having their fur conditioned with oil. It might have been the one thing the two animals could agree upon.

"Dirty beast," Ting said, laughing, patting Aejej's dusty rump.

I looked at Tende and smirked, remembering how Dedan and I first met him. Dirty beast, indeed.

As night fell, we headed back to Ssolu. The sunset was beautiful. Our bellies were full, as we'd bartered for some street food in the market before leaving. The silence between us gave me a chance to think. All this time, The Cleanser had been taking from the Osu-nu people. Every Adoro village endured The Cleanser. It came and took and now I knew what it took. It was taking those of us destined to do something, something great or small, bad or good, *something*. It was flattening us as a people. Shaving away our peaks and dips. Then it sent them back with a cheap gift—beauty, attractiveness, the gift of allure, popularity. This was the "cleanse." Then that person would marry well, have the respect and adoration of the community, the envy of their peers . . . cheap gifts at a great great cost. I didn't know *how* The Cleanser stole destiny. Maybe that answer was written on the paper, maybe it wasn't. That didn't matter to me as much as how to kill it.

"We're about an hour from Ssolu," Ting said, hours later.

"So we stop here?" I asked. We both knew why.

"Yes. This is as good a place as any."

We set up camp, and I built a fire while Ting used our capture station to collect water for Aejej and Tende. When they were settled, we sat down before the fire and looked at each other. I fidgeted with Dedan's blue prism a bit, enjoying the feel of its perfect smooth glass edges and looking through it at the firelight. Then I placed it inside my pocket and reached into the pouch beside me. Carefully, I brought out the piece of paper and we began.

This was mystical work, so I cannot describe it fully to you.

Ting was younger than me, but she'd been working and mastering the Mystic Points for decades longer than I. And her strongest Mystic Point, like my Onyesonwu's and Aro's, was the Uwa Point, the most material point. But the direction she moved was not toward the body, it was to one of the most physical manifestations of mysticism, the script of nsibidi. She could read what was on the paper. I could read some nsibidi, but my knowledge was nothing close to her mastery.

"Do you know what it said on that iron gate in the Paper House?" she asked as I allowed my eyes to lightly glance at the paper.

I didn't look directly at the symbols, but already they were pulling at my mind. It sparked a gentle pain and gave me a distant anxiety. "What did it say?" I muttered.

"I could not read the name of the masquerade who wrote it, but that gate is a surveillance device of the wilderness. Whomever walks under it is *seen* by the one who wrote it."

"Who?" I asked. I was vaguely listening.

"I don't know," she said. "The nsibidi was written

like a series of tight impossible knots that got smaller and smaller as I read it. It may have even gotten microscopic. Even one of those powerful portables that can magnify may not have been able to see it."

Microscopic nsibidi? I could barely concentrate on the idea. She took the paper from me. "That's enough, let me see," she said. "My turn."

I frowned, but I was deeply relieved that she'd taken it from me. I exhaled, sitting back.

She sniffed the paper and shook it a bit as she spoke, "The gate wasn't even from your village, it was from a town called Nesh. Carried on the backs of five camels who all died when they arrived in Adoro 5."

"Nesh?" I asked. "That is not an Osu-nu town."

She shrugged, touching the paper to her tongue. She grimaced. "It could easily have been made long before there was an Osu-nu people." She was looking at the paper, scowling. She ran a hand over it and then stood up. "One does not stand in one spot to watch a masquerade," she said. "You get up, too."

She brought out her portable and played a drum-heavy beat. We danced for an hour. There was music from the portable, in my head and in the desert, the storm of Ssolu not far away, so it wasn't strange. Nsibidi is not only written, it is "played," it is pantomimed.

What is written is also spoken with the movement of the body. The written, the spoken, and the danced were fluid. Not long before the sun rose, the masquerade rose from the dry cracked earth. In the waning shadows, it pushed up, clouds of dirt and stone tumbling as it emerged. It brought its own music.

Ting turned off her portable, but the drumming and reedy flute continued. As we danced, we read. Ting guided the way, but we both took in the information. And it needed to be that way because, though Ting was the one with the mastery to read the complex nsibidi, it was most necessary for me to understand it.

What the paper said was that The Cleanser was old. "Cleanser" was not even its name. Its name was something from the wilderness that I could not even think, let alone pronounce. And it was not of Ani. It cleaned what was not meant to be clean. Why it sprang into the physical world was beyond both of our understanding. It was not for us to know. I was comfortable with not knowing everything; I understood that mystery was sometimes necessary, but this time it annoyed me. To destroy it was to change the world and bring natural mystery, unpredictability and awe back to it. It would turn the fourth Mystic Point . . . cleanse those who shouldn't be clean, it is a spirit, and it is many and one. This was what Ting and I read and understood from that circular piece of paper the overseer had allowed us to take. However, my greatest question was not answered by what was written.

The masquerade was over twenty feet tall now. Gently bouncing as it grew and grew. Black smoke rolled down its sides, the sand absorbing it like water. It smelled of dust and but also the sweat of a large anxious man. Looking at it burned my eyes and blurred my vision the way the salt from sweat does.

"Oooh, Ani is great," Ting whispered.

I nodded.

"I have not met many of them," she said. For the first time since I'd met her, she looked afraid.

"I have," I said.

"Onyesonwu told me she met a big one on her journey here," Ting said.

My heart fluttered. I needed to ask her more about my daughter. Much more. But for now, I had to focus. Its thirty-foot body was now fully emerged. The masquerade was the size of a house and vaguely shaped like a baobab tree with tendrils of smoke branching out from the top and then falling like foam. Its smoke tumbled to and disappeared at our feet.

"They seem to like me," I said. "That's what Aro says."

Ting moved behind me and I smiled. I was afraid, but there are times when I feel that I am precisely where I am supposed to be. I felt this way now. This masquerade could erase both me and Ting on a whim. We'd called it by reading about The Cleanser, and maybe even by my walking under the iron gate in the Paper House. This was part of the nsibidi. And this masquerade was angry. I stepped up to it on shaky legs.

CHAPTER 8

Study

Masquerades are spirits from the wilderness. Most have never been alive and do not want to be. They come in all types of manifestations when they visit the physical world. They are often trees, great and small beasts. They can be hills that weren't there before. Puffs of smoke, fire, burning bales of hay. Undulating dancing things made of colorful light, insects, raffia, mud, woven yarn. So many things. I know them when I see them. They make it known when they want to be seen. Ah, they are difficult to explain.

But some masquerades were once alive. Ancestors. They always remember. Their agendas remain human. The most harmful masquerades tend to be of this type. And their harm is always specific, to a people, to a place, to an idea, to a point in time.

"You cannot turn back," it said.

We were alone. In its darkness. Only I glowed in

my kponyungo form. If I didn't glow, it would have consumed me. Thankfully, I am who I am. "I don't intend to."

"Those who play don't survive."

"Do not take Ting's life," I said. As I have said, I have dealt with many masquerades. I know how they think.

"Why?"

"She played in my place. View us as one."

It said nothing.

"I cannot interpret the nsibidi. She can. But I need to know it. I am an Osu-nu sorcerer. My people are The Cleanser's target. I am not just one seeking information. I am not a scholar who's gone too far with her studies. These are my people."

"Najeeba," it said. Hearing it speak my name was alarming. I stood up straighter. **"The Cleanser crossed over on a bridge of guilt, insecurity, failure. Human things. From back then, from back there. It locates and robs those who show potential. It takes their power and gives back something that looks like power but is actually quite useless. In this way, it keeps the Osu-nu people even, controlled, and unremarkable."**

"I know this, but why?"

"It has become the bridge that allowed its existence, the spirit is body, it was inevitable."

"So it was a mistake?"

"If that sets your furious mind at ease."

"It doesn't."

"What is it you want, Najeeba?"

"I want to kill it. Tell me how to kill it. It. Has. Wronged. Me." I was trembling and absolutely blazing with rage now.

"In thirty-two nights, it will come," it said. **"You have done it before. You cannot know how to do it. Find it. If you don't kill it, it will kill you. Knowing how to do something is not always the answer."**

Done what before? It was speaking in riddles and smoke as masquerades so often did. I needed a clearer explanation. I couldn't quite grasp what it was saying. But I knew not to ask a masquerade to clarify itself. I'd done this once to a small one that had appeared to me as a cactus in my cactus candy garden. "What is your point?" I'd asked it, annoyed. It was a rotted looking cactus giggling amongst my prized plants, and this had annoyed me. It had shot ten thorns into my hands. They'd been itchy for weeks as the wounds healed.

If I had asked this great beast what it meant by

what it had told me, it may have simply killed both me and Ting . . . wherever Ting was. So I stayed silent as it pulled me into its blackness. Whirling and swirling around me, leaving me smelling unwashed and stressed. I was back in the desert at our small camp. Our fire had been blown out. Ting stood there staring at me.

"Najeeba," she breathed. She coughed. "Are you all right?" Then she fell to her knees, coughing some more.

I tried to get up. "Ting," I gasped. Then I felt something pressing hard on my chest. My temples thudded. The world went silver blue red. "What's happening?" I thickly asked. Everything went black.

I smelled smoke. The smoldering embers of our fire. I was on my back. I turned to the side. Ting was still lying where she'd fallen. Slowly, I sat up, joints popping, muscles twitching, lower back aching, eyes stinging. How long had I been there? It was still night, barely. The same night? I surveyed the area. Aejej paced and nickered yards away; Tende stood a bit closer but in the other direction, frozen with fear.

"Ting?" I said. My throat was so dry. I coughed.

She didn't respond.

I dragged myself to my feet. My breasts were painfully engorged. Oh my knees ached horribly. I stumbled to her. "Ting," I said louder. I gently nudged her with my sandaled foot. I had a flashback of decades ago, in The Before, when I'd kicked Teka as she lay in the sand trying to die after we'd all been assaulted by those Nuru men out there in the desert. After the assault by Daib that gave me my daughter Onyesonwu. Where it happened, outside of the town of Sangerfut, was not far from where we were. I'd nudged and then shaken Teka, and she'd finally responded by croaking two words that I will remember forever, "Leave me." I tried to pull her up and she wouldn't move. She said it again, "Leave me." I will never know if Teka ever got up.

I shut my eyes and rubbed my forehead, trying to push away the memory, all the gruesome memories from that day trying to flood into my conscious mind. I shuddered and shoved Ting harder with my foot. "*Ting*!" I screamed.

"Hmmm?"

I gasped with relief, falling to the ground beside her. "Get up."

"I will," she muttered, her eyes still closed. "I'm just . . . trying to gather myself."

I helped push her upright. Her eyes shot open. "Oh!" She jumped to her feet.

"What?!" I said, falling back. "What is it?"

She ran off, pulling down and kicking off her now very dusty white pants in a singular motion. She squatted. I turned away as she urinated a powerful stream that went on for nearly a minute. How long had we been out? I looked at my dirty white dress. No urine. I felt the need to urinate, but nothing so urgent. No blood, either. I did feel the front of my shirt dampening as my breasts began to leak. I expressed some of it to relieve the pain. I wanted to be full for Sssolu.

When Ting finished, she came back to me, looking more like herself. "I'm glad that my calling has always been nsibidi. Masquerades are awful."

We coaxed Aejej and Tende back to us, packed up, and continued on our way. We had bags of groundnuts and dates but none of us wanted to eat, not even Aejej and Tende. The two seemed a bit traumatized.

Aejej wouldn't let me touch him and Tende wouldn't let me walk more than a few feet from him. I understood. No living thing would be the same after setting eyes on a masquerade, especially one like that in close proximity.

"We probably shouldn't have had them so close to us when we played the nsibidi," I said.

"You couldn't have led them far enough to not be affected by that," Ting said, patting Aejej on the neck. I could see him looking at me with the side of his eye, still suspicious.

It turned out that we'd been out for an hour and sunrise was minutes away. We were both exhausted but neither of us wanted to stay a moment longer where that masquerade had been. Ting folded up the piece of paper and put it in the envelope. Neither of us planned to ever touch it again, but maybe her teacher Ssaiku would want to inspect it.

"Thirty-two nights," I said. "That's the real information it gave me. I know when it's coming."

"But not where it'll be."

"I think I can find it when it comes to Adoro 5," I said. As the kponyungo, it would be simple. I'd been able to sense it last time, even from Jwahir. "The question is, what will I do when I find it. The masquerade said I'd done it before."

Ting only shook her head. "They speak in proverbs, I hate it. Just like typical elders."

I was used to it. It was best not to try too hard. To just let the words wash over me. And to wait. I had to wait.

═

We arrived at Ssolu three hours later. My breasts felt like they would explode. Ting brought down the storm. Once we were at the edge of the village, she brought it back up. We sat on the sand for a half hour as everything settled and Ting rested. All of Ssolu knew we'd returned when they saw the storm go down and up. Dedan and Sssolu were waiting in our tent for me when I entered it. The three of us saw no one until the sun rose the next day. Sssolu fed well that evening, and I slept like the dead.

CHAPTER 9

Dedan

Dedan was different.

"Why are you smiling so much?" I asked, as soon as we were alone in our tent. Sssolu was asleep. Dedan's smile was contagious.

He reached out and touched my cheek, "I'm so glad you're back," he said.

"So am I."

"But I'm still angry."

"I assumed."

We fell into each other's arms and soon we were intertwined on the mat. Sssolu was fast asleep, so we were able to focus fully on each other. I breathed as I wrapped my legs around him and arched my back. I exhaled and gently left my body, floating slowly up to the top of the tent, becoming the kponyungo. I looked down at myself, at Dedan, who moaned below me with pleasure. I was about to fly off when I happened to look to the left, near Sssolu's basket.

A masquerade stood beside it. It was about four feet tall, humanoid, with green slender arms and legs and a purple raffia puff around its neck. It had a wooden green head, but no face.

"No!" I roared, flying right back into my body. Dedan gasped and softly gagged as he climaxed inside me and I shook my head trying to force myself to return. I wanted to roll off Dedan and run to my daughter, but a climax rushed from between my legs, up my spine and radiated across my chest like electricity. We were in this state for several moments before I managed to turn my head and crawl off him toward Sssolu.

"What, what are you doing?" Dedan breathed. "Are you alright?"

I was halfway across the tent when I stopped. There was nothing there. No masquerade. Sssolu was still fast asleep. I collapsed on my belly and let out a sigh. "I . . . saw something. Near Sssolu," I said.

"From . . . above?" he asked.

I nodded. I pressed my face to the ground. "Oh Ani," I whispered. I looked up just to make sure.

With my woman's eyes, I saw nothing. But with my kponyungo eyes, I was sure I'd see it.

"Who did you see?" he asked.

Not what. Who. I looked at him. "You're different."

He smiled brilliantly. "I am."

"Why?" I sat up slowly.

"You weren't the only one who found something over the last few days."

"Something good?"

He nodded. "Oh, Jeeb. It was right that I left Jwahir and came with you. Good for you, good for me, good for our daughter Sssolu." He sat up. "They love her here, so much. Ah, I have so much to tell you . . . my mouth isn't big enough."

"I've never seen you so happy," I said, grinning back at him. I got up, joined him on the mat, and let him take me into his arms. I'd felt good since returning, but now I was conscious of why. The joy he exuded warmed me like sunshine in the desert morning.

"You want me to tell you?"

"Yes. What happened. Tell me."

"Right now?"

"Yes, right now."

He touched the side of my face. "I got answers, Jeeb," he whispered. "All of them. *All of them.*"

There is nothing like hearing a story of unexpected joy from someone you love. When I left with Ting, I didn't expect Dedan to do more than worry about me. He'd been beside himself when I told him what I wanted to do and that he had to stay behind with our daughter. Even if he'd wanted to follow me, he could not because of the storm. He was afraid that he'd never see me again. He knew I was capable of getting myself killed. "You want to kill that thing more than you want to live," he'd said. "I know you. You have this drive. You need that end, even if it ends you."

I'd assured him that I would come back, then I'd added, "Even if I come back as an Alusi." That did not amuse him. The last thing he wanted to imagine me as was a desert spirit, wandering, traveling, exploring forever. We'd argued over it well into the night and then he'd gone somewhere early in the morning. Then I'd left with Ting as both he and I knew I would. That night, Ssaiku asked him to dinner. This dinner turned out to be a meeting with two others. When he told me who they were, I was stunned. And not because one of the men was Sola, the sorcerer who initiated me and taught me so much.

"They came for Sssolu," Dedan said.

"Why?" I nearly shouted. I was on my feet and my noise woke Sssolu up. She started crying. Dedan wrapped a red wrapper around his waist and went to her. I watched him for a moment, my mind reeling. The night after I'd left the village, they'd shown up. Sola and the sorcerer I'd met only once when I was a child on the evening just after I'd nearly been attacked at the market.

"You sure his name was Cat?" I asked, as Dedan picked up Sssolu. He cradled her to him. I slipped into my red night dress and sat on the mat.

"Yes," he said. "And, yes, he is the one you are thinking of. He said he was. Who was he?"

"What did he look like? He must be quite old. He was old when *I* saw him back then!"

"I don't know, he looked . . . no older than Aro."

I held my arms up and he put Sssolu in them. She cooed, calming down. I sat on the mat with her, and Dedan joined me.

"He didn't explain to you how I knew him?"

"He said he gave you water."

"He . . . he did something, and my brothers and

father couldn't move," I said, remembering. I'd been terrified of this Nuru man with his gaunt face and juju. "Then he walked up to me and said something like, 'They gave you a lesson. Let's hope you learned it.' Then he put his hand on my face and something electric . . . shot from it and hit me square in the forehead." I would never forget it. Whatever it was felt wet and it hurt a little. I could never say this to Dedan, but there was something sexual about it. There'd been a penetration. I remember it left me feeling dirty. Violated. I'd later taken a bath, scrubbing and scrubbing my skin. "Gave me 'water.'" I repeated, my lip curling with disgust.

"'I was there when your Najeeba sold a dangerous cube of salt. It went on to grow an entire forest.' Did you know that it—?"

"No," I snapped.

Dedan told me the rest as I rocked Sssolu back to sleep. Sola and Cat had come to see our daughter. Ssaiku had brought them to her. Dedan didn't know if they knew I was leaving and had timed Sola and Cat's arrival in the village just so. He didn't ask. And when Dedan dined with the three of them, Sola and Cat had barely been curious about him, more interested in seeing Sssolu after the meal.

And then Sola asked him about the leather cord with the blue piece of glass he wore around his neck. When Dedan told them about the glass house, he felt their attention shift to him, and it was so sharp that he had been a little afraid.

The three men already made him nervous. When Ssaiku had invited him to dinner, he'd nearly said no. If anything, he'd gone out of fear of what would happen to him if he declined the invitation. When he met Sola and Cat, he'd felt like fleeing. He was used to me. I didn't scare him because he knew I loved him. And he knew every side of me. He understood me, even those things that were unfathomable. But these three men were not only powerful, confident, and knowing, but they were old, and strange. When they focused on him, he felt it would burn him to ash.

But when he told them about the glass house, something in him blazed. He felt fortified and empowered by all that he'd known when he had the idea, when he'd built it, when Jwahir had exhaled and felt healed, and then when he needed to destroy it. Those things he could never put words to were his, they made him who he was. The split in him was his to own. The knowing despite the fact that he could never know. The itch he could never scratch. The pain he could never relive. The Before he did not remember, even when I told him about it. It slipped from his memory and direct understanding. And the result of that split. The juju of it.

Ssaiku, Sola, and Cat had crowded around him, asking him question after question.

"Why are you wearing that earring?"

"Where did you come from?"

"Why do you work with glass?"

"Let me see your necklace."

"What do you think of the Great Book?"

"What does the discomfort feel like?"

"When you built the house, what did you see in your mind's eye?"

"You love Najeeba?"

"Who is your mother?"

"Have you ever walked in your sleep?"

They asked these questions with fascination, curiosity, concern, and—this is his words not mine . . . love. Dedan said the sorcerers were loving in their concern. I had a hard time believing this. Dedan could be emotional and empathetic. He may have read things in their behavior that were not there. Love? From old sorcerers? I don't know that they are capable of that, and I know their type better than he does. But then again, Dedan was a man as they both were.

He answered all their questions, and they asked him even more. For hours. He talked until his voice grew hoarse. But it felt great. Like the poison was bleeding from him, clearing and opening passageways so he could draw something light and sweet in.

When he told the sorcerers of this feeling, Cat had said his "doors were opening." By this time, it was near sunrise. They went to the outer part of the village, at the border of the storm. As they walked, Dedan had asked them why they had not gone to see Sssolu, as that was the reason they had come. They said they would greet Sssolu in the morning.

"We danced," Dedan said. He was smiling now and tears welled in his eyes. "One of them began a chant and . . ." He trailed off, shaking his head. I just stared at him. A deep memory was coming back to me, and I didn't want to move for fear that the spell would break and the memory would pull away.

I was back at that cave. My father was alive. So many miles away, my mother was alive. A fire was burning and father and my brothers were gathered around it. I lay on a mat in the cave, listening to them sing wildly. Stamping their feet. Old songs. Timeless spirit. The last time my family was truly happy, whole, and healthy.

"As we sang, the sun began to rise behind the storm's wall," Dedan continued. He got up and stood over me. "You can see it, you know. Just so. The storm is a juju storm, it is but a veil. I was the only one singing after a while. I saw Ssaiku draw something in the sand, but I turned my back to him and sang to the sun rising, an orange disk emerging from the sand. Slowly. Rising. Oh, it was mighty. All knowing."

He described the sun like it was a masquerade.

"Ani is great," I whispered.

He nodded. "Then, it was like I . . . was looking at myself. I was standing before me. A different me . . ." He trailed off, a distant look on his face. Dedan could not tell me anymore. I didn't ask it of him. He'd met himself from The Before, maybe. Did he embrace himself? Absorb himself? Watch himself disappear? Blow away? Walk away? Whatever he did, it freed him. And he was so happy.

I was envious.

CHAPTER 10

No One Above Me

And that broke something between us.

I wasn't free. I had something to kill. I couldn't rest until this was done. My father's sister had been taken and returned by The Cleanser. What had The Cleanser taken from her? What was it she was supposed to have done? I'd never know. But then she fell in love with a non-Osu-nu, and when the family found out about their love, it had risen up and killed her and my father's entire family. Whatever The Cleanser had done caused a ripple effect that left my father cowering in that Adoro temple begging Adoro, Ani, whomever would listen, to allow him revenge.

I was his revenge.

I wouldn't be free until I killed The Cleanser.

Dedan had faced his challenge and now he was nothing but joy. He was clean. I loved being around him and Sssolu. When I was with them, I didn't think much about what I had to do. On top of this, Dedan was changing. I saw it one day when he was with Ssolu. She was fussing a bit while he was talking to someone and without even thinking about it, he held his hand over her face and I could see a soft orange yellow glow just beneath his palm. Sssolu immediately calmed. The Vah worked minor jujus naturally, it wasn't taught or discussed. It was just something they did, like talking or laughing. They could attract bees to hives by singing, draw away flies by blowing the air, cool a stew by sticking a fingertip in it, they could hear each other over the storm when it was an emergency. Small things. Dedan had started to do them, too.

And Dedan became a full glassmaker again. No surprise there. Over our months of travel, he talked about it often. I'd find him gazing at a handful of sand in the sun. Fiddling with his necklace constantly, running his thumb over the edges of its blue glass. It was only a matter of time. He'd made friends with two women who baked bread and they helped him find the materials he needed to build a kiln– some clay bricks and large stones. He used camel dung for fuel and to fire it the high winds near the edge of the village for bellows. And there was plenty of sand, soda ash and limestone. When Ting walked up to me sipping tea from a blue glass cup, I knew the entire village was probably using all kinds of new glass items.

Dedan was becoming one of the Red People. Sssolu was already one of them. I barely saw her. Villagers, mostly women, a few men, would take her for days at a time. Children would bring her gifts and sing songs about her. There was a village meeting where a whole five minutes was dedicated to welcoming her and officially speaking her name, "Sssoluuuuu!" That evening, Dedan sat with Ssaiku and some other men. I was to sit with Ting, but I chose to stay near the back, mixed in with those who did not hold great importance in the community.

By those last few days that's how things had been. I saw less and less of Sssolu and Dedan. We spent our nights together, though Sssolu was often in someone else's tent. Over the weeks, she gained weight and her hair got bushier. She was so beautiful. A noisy, fussy, happy baby who drank from both me and some of the other women in the village. Was I okay with all of this? The Vah are not a people who own their children. It is a village of love. Even husband and wives shared their beds with others on occasion and without judgment. I believe Dedan had been with one or two other Vah women. I had several offers, too, though I didn't take anyone up on them. This did not diminish my bond with Dedan. Children were free to roam, they were safe, fed, taught at many homes. This was the Vah. And so, no, the fact that Sssolu was the entire village's daughter did not bother me.

I spent more and more time alone during the day. Dedan and baby Sssolu were always surrounded by people. Only when I nursed her did I get time alone with Sssolu and only when we were intimate did I get time fully alone with Dedan. I smiled and thought of my mother who loved her solitude so much. I was becoming more like her. I preferred it this way because the time was getting close, and I felt more and more anxious. I spent hours on the outskirts, seated in the sand facing the storm while I flew as the kponyungo. I burst through the storm into the quiet of the desert where I'd fly low over the sand dunes. Out there, I was at peace, in the moment. It helped that I knew Dedan and Sssolu were cared for and happy.

I'd land on the sand and take my human form and walk in the sun. Once in a while, I'd see a lizard. They were aware of me but not afraid when I was in this form. Some of them would turn and come to me, trying to crawl up my legs. They learned that there were limits to their will. During these times alone, I would think about what I'd learned about The Cleanser. My knowledge was so limited. I knew its actions and consequences, I vaguely knew its origin, but what could I expect when I finally encountered it? Would it be in physical or spirit form? Would it be sentient? Individual? Or part of many or a greater whole? And what would happen if I tried to kill it? If . . . *when* I succeeded.

I would succeed.

In these days, I missed Aro. I longed to sit before Sola's fire and hear him speak at me. My teachers. Those elders above you upon whose chests you could rest your head. But Sola had come for my daughter; he hadn't stayed to see me. And Aro was far away, maybe he did not travel as Sola could or didn't want to. I missed my father and my mother. I felt orphaned. I was truly a master now. There was no one above me.

The night before the thirty second day, I woke up beside Dedan. Sssolu was in my arms and in the glow from Dedan's portable's nightlight, I could see that she was wide awake. She'd grown a lot but she was still an infant. So elemental. But, praise be to Ani, our Sssolu could see into me. Maybe this was why an entire village had immediately claimed her. And maybe some other reasons, too. Sssolu was a beacon. She shined so brightly, a child who could have only come from me. She had Dedan's nose, mouth, forehead, and hair, but she was all me.

She held me with her eyes, her tiny head tilted up. She was calm, breathing deeply. I sat up quiet and leaned over her. She followed my face and I nodded. "You have my attention," I said.

She wore a gown woven from very finely braided raffia that had been washed and washed to softness. Sssolu spent most of her time in this gown. Ting had drawn and "pushed" a tiny protective nsibidi symbol on the chest. I didn't know what it meant, but I trusted her. I touched the symbol with my finger. "Ikuku," I whispered to her. It was not her name but it was the name I'd given her. She grasped my thumb. Tears stung my eyes as I spoke the words from my heart that I never wanted to speak aloud, "You don't need me." My chest hitched, and I reached for her with my other hand. "But I need you." Tears dripped onto her gown and still she was calm, watching me.

She was calm, so I would be calm. I inhaled and exhaled. Steadied. Her large dark brown eyes were black in the soft dim light. I don't know if she grasped my thumb harder, but I imagine she did. I held her closer to me and became the kponyungo. Her gaze followed me as I hovered above her. She cooed, her arms and legs working. I descended closer, my flames lighting her face. I glanced around our tent and there, less than two feet from us, was the masquerade. I hadn't checked for it since that first time, afraid of what I'd see and preferring to be in a sort of denial.

But there it was. Without the element of surprise, I didn't fear it. My daughter had attracted a whole village, this masquerade was simply another who she attracted. In time, she'd probably attract more of them.

"I do see you," I told it.

Ever so slightly, it shook. But that was all. Acknowledgement.

I turned back to my daughter and brought my spirit face to her tiny one. She looked . . . she glowed, like me. Oh Ani, my daughter was so like me. We gazed into each other's eyes and then it was like she blew something at me with them. Green. So much green. I had to fight to stay where I was. It was jarring, and I wasn't used to feeling this way while in this state. I dropped back into my body. Then I was sniffing and looking around. I looked at my night clothes, and then I pressed them to my face and inhaled. I smelled her. My Onyesonwu.

"Ikuku, did you . . ." I smelled my clothes again. It had been so long since I had smelled her. I silently burst into tears, getting to my feet. I looked at Dedan. He was still fast asleep. My face was wet with sweat and tears. So much loss. So many gone. So many left behind. I was like an Alusi already. A desert spirit who's only purpose was to travel, see, manifest, and remember.

When I looked at my daughter, she'd gone back to sleep on the mat. Peaceful as ever. I lay back beside her, Dedan on the other side. He muttered something about glass fish on iron tables and put an arm around my waist. I pressed it to me, cradled Sssolu and shut my eyes. I could still smell Onyesonwu on me; somehow Sssolu had brought her spirit to me for just a moment. And then I, too, fell into a peaceful sleep.

CHAPTER 11

Alone

Dust and wind.

Then the storm was behind me, and I was back in Ssolu. I flew up, the tents of the Vah below me. Higher. The winds here picked up, the air was cooler and refreshing because even the sheets of dust from the storm could not reach this high. I drifted, watching the recently risen sun. A bright sharp orange as it hovered just at the horizon. As the kponyungo, I could look directly at the sun and in doing so it looked more like the star it was. Glowing, roiling, its tart orange more illusion than fact.

Slowly, I began to descend, letting all my anxieties and excitement drift from me. By the time I reached my body sitting on the sand before the storm. I felt so peaceful that the transition from spirit to physical was seamless. I sighed, gently opening my eyes.

"That was beautiful to witness."

I jumped. Ting was sitting beside me.

"I made myself ignorable," she explained. "You didn't even see me with your other eyes. I'm that good."

I tried to shake myself into better awareness, but it was difficult. I'd been flying for hours. "What do you want?" I muttered. I felt a little guilty about leaving Sssolu and Dedan so early to come out here and Ting seeing me out here exacerbated my guilt.

She shrugged, bringing a small white stick from her pocket. She blew a spark from between her fingers to light it. She took a deep pull from it, inhaled and slowly let out the smoke. It smelled sweet and light. She held it out to me. I took it and looked at it and then took a puff.

"I wanted to speak to you before you left."

I blew out smoke. "Ah, you've been counting the days, too."

"Of course, I have."

I took another puff deep into my lungs. I shut my eyes as I felt its soft wave ripple through me. "Would you rather me stay? Forget about my mission to kill The Cleanser? Become a Vah woman of Ssolu, your sister in sorcery?"

Ting laughed. "You'll never be one of us."

I shot a look at her. Then I chuckled. She was right.

"I asked Ssaiku about this. That is what he told me."

"Ah, Ssaiku. He doesn't like me," I said.

"That doesn't make him wrong."

"What of Dedan?" I asked.

"Yes. He already is one of us."

"Sssolu?"

"She will not only be Vah, she . . . you've brought us . . . what The Cleanser would want to take."

"Who will be her teacher?" I asked. I was not stupid.

"Me," Ting said.

"I didn't ask for Sssolu to be a sorcerer, though."

"There are times where it is just so," Ting said.

I nodded. At least Cat would not be her teacher.

"Your daughter *will* see Cat again," Ting said, as if reading my thoughts.

I scoffed. "I don't want to leave them." I handed the stick back to her and she took one more puff and ground it into the sand. "You know what I realized? Do you remember how I told you my father died? After encountering those dead things on the salt roads, after finding that strange cube?"

"Yes."

"I had kind of hoped to go and see if I could kill those, too—"

"They weren't alive," Ting said.

"That is true, but also, Onyesonwu cured them. They would not be there anymore."

"Ah, because she cured the Great Book."

"Yes. My daughter did so much."

"Do you know how you'll . . . do it?"

"No."

"Are you afraid?"

"I'm only afraid to face it, to see it. What will it really look like? How will it be?"

"You will know by this time tomorrow, if that helps. The wait is almost over."

I shivered.

"I'm glad to have met you," Ting suddenly said. "I knew you were an extraordinary person when I met your daughter. From the moment I saw her, I wondered what kind of woman could birth her. She was truly remarkable. Brash, impulsive, willful, and so courageous and durable. She could make anything happen by sheer will. The mother of such a girl, I wanted to meet her . . . you."

"I'm just a woman," I muttered. Her words were making me want to jump out of my skin. I knew I was extraordinary. My father had asked it to be so, and I had cultivated my father's wishes. But it was another thing to hear it from someone else, for someone else who was like me to see me. I didn't like it. It made what I had to do in a few hours that much more inevitable.

"No, you're not," she snapped. "Stop it. And I put nsibidi on both of her hands."

"What?"

"Her father cursed her with cruel poison, and I had to chase it out of her like an insect," she said. "Drawing into her skin to force it out. Then it jumped and a priest stepped on it. But when I was finished, her hands were both tattooed." She paused, about to say more. She shut her mouth.

"She was okay?"

"Eventually, yes. By the time she left Ssolu, she was changed, stronger, ready. Your daughter."

"Am I ready?"

She looked at me for a long time. "I don't know," she finally said. "Do you think you are?"

"The Cleanser comes tomorrow."

"It does."

"Will Dedan be alright?" I asked.

"He will thrive here," she said. "But . . . he came here for you."

"Should I go to see Ssaiku and the chief and chieftess?"

"That is not necessary."

I smiled. Good. I hated goodbyes.

"I will bring down the storm in three hours," she said. "We will be packing up and moving on in three days."

My family.

First I went to Tende and MorningStar. They were with other camels, but resting in their own little spot. They sniffed at me, and MorningStar groaned lovingly nudging me with her head. I stumbled a bit from that and laughed. "I am going and you are both staying," I said. I sighed. "We've come a long way." I'd journeyed into death and back with MorningStar and Tende had been saved by Dedan. Into MorningStar's ear, I whispered, "Sssssssolu. I named her Ikuku. Dedan named her The Wind." MorningStar hummed deep in her throat, a sound I'd never heard her make. I rested my head on her neck, and she did it again. Tende gently bit my shoulder and then nudged me along. "I'll make you proud," I said to him. As I walked past Aejej, he nickered and went into his stable. He still hadn't gotten over seeing me speak to a masquerade.

I went to find Dedan and Sssolu. The hours were ours. I won't dwell on those two goodbyes. I can't stand it. Dedan could not bear to let go of me, and I had to roughly pull his arms from me and twist my body to get away from him. Sssolu . . . the women took her away as I fell to my knees, silent, not weeping. I don't cry for my beautiful baby. Loved and cherished by a whole village.

When sunset arrived, after I'd spent hours saying goodbye to the two most important people to me in this world, I left.

I left.

I left.

I left.

CHAPTER 12

Men's Club

I stood outside of Ssolu eating a piece of cactus candy. A woman cultivated them in Ssolu. Hers were nowhere near as good as mine, but cactus candy is cactus candy. Rarely is it not tasty. I was waiting for Ting to bring the storm up. Within minutes, she did. I stayed there for a while. Within less than a minute, the village of Ssolu was no longer in view. I was on the outside now. Alone. I turned, hoisted up my small pack and walked to my childhood home. Back to Adoro 5.

I arrived not long before sunset. The masquerade had said The Cleanser would come in the night. In all the stories I heard, this meant quite late. The child it chose always disappeared from their home when everyone was asleep. It was this way for my father's sister. I'd never thought to ask how long she was gone or how she came back. There was so much I didn't know.

In the market was a men's club where men went at the end of the day to drink palm wine and beer and laugh and talk. Though it was unacceptable for girls and women, I'd always wanted to go with my father. He'd come home from meetings and excursions, and I'd be so excited to spend time with him, but then he'd leave for the men's club and come back another hour later and spend the rest of the evening with my mother and me. I understood that this was his social time, but I wanted to be a part of that, too.

I'd had the courage to tell him about having the Call, but I'd never had enough courage to ask him to bring me with. And he'd have certainly never brought me along. My brothers asked often, and he never allowed them until they were in their late 20s. Now as I walked toward the market, I wondered if the place was where it had been in The Before.

I strolled along the side of the road with women returning from the market or going to the night market. A few of them glanced at me. I was wearing a loose red dress woven from washed and softened dyed palm fibers given to me by the Vah. The material didn't flow like the silk and cotton garments of the people of Adoro 5. I knew I looked different. I chuckled to myself, "I've been gone for too long." Regardless, I carried myself with confidence, greeting the women around me politely. Setting them at ease. Three women walked with me for a bit, occasionally glancing at me. They were eating groundnuts and they offered me some. "Thank you," I said, taking some.

"Your dress is very interesting," one of them said, looking at me from the side of her eye.

"Good for travel," I said, shelling a groundnut and popping it in my mouth. Then I added, "It's nice to be home."

"Oh? You're from Adoro 5?" another woman asked. She might had been about my age. It was too dark to see her clearly.

"Yes," I said.

"Born here?"

I hesitated. "Yes."

"Welcome home," she said and I breathed a sigh of relief. I had too much to do today to get stuck explaining myself to someone who may have recognized me. When I reached the market, it was so busy,

I could just blend in. I walked slowly, taking it all in. It hadn't changed much. People sold just about everything at their booths, the day sellers replaced by the night sellers. From glass works to vegetables to electronics to cooking utensils, everything you could imagine. I'd never spent a lot of time in the market, so I couldn't tell how different it was, if different at all. There were a few salt sellers owned by Osu-nu people selling to Nurus and non-Osu-nu. This was a difference I could point out. In The Before, where everyone here was Osu-nu and thus all sellers of salt, there was no need for such sellers here.

I found the men's club more easily than I expected. I simply followed the general flow of things. There were men all over the place, but they generally moved in one direction. I observed this current and followed it. The men's club was a large booth with wooden stools and tables and chairs. The ground was covered with fragrant smelling wood shavings and the tables each had bowls of shelled groundnuts on them.

I hesitated and then boldly walked into the space. I sat at a stool, ignoring the gaze of several of the men around me. I had time to kill before I killed something terrible, I dared one of them to come up to me and tell me not to spend it here. But though they stared, none did. And after several minutes, the stares gradually decreased and then mostly stopped all together. A man came up and offered me a cup of palm wine or beer. I took a cup of palm wine.

"Thank you," I said, looking him in the eye.

He moved on quickly, clearly uncomfortable. As I looked around, I realized that I could no longer be sure if Osu-nu people were still considered "untouchable." My father's family had been killed because his sister had fallen in love with a non-Osu-nu Okeke man. Did that kind of thing even happen anymore? No. Adoro 5 was different. But it still had its Cleanser.

One man would not stop staring at me. He was sitting on a stool with some other men, two Okeke and two Nuru. A tall dark-skinned man with a well-kept salt and pepper beard. He wore a rich blue caftan and pants and he had palm fiber rings on each finger. Clearly an Osu-nu man of status.

I stared back at him. For over two minutes, neither of us broke the gaze. Finally, he frowned and got up, still holding my gaze. As he walked over, I considered the various ways I could hurt him if he tried anything. The one I settled on was *ndbe abum obbaw,* which means, "leopard knocks his foot." An old juju from more lush and green times created by a sorceress to stop a leopard from attacking her. It would make this man knock his foot hard on something that would cause such pain he'd become incapacitated. Easy to work and very effective.

He sat across from me at my table. "Najeeba," he said.

I blinked and frowned. "How do you know my—?" He grinned, and I gasped recognizing him. "Obi!"

"When did you return?" he asked. "I thought I'd never see you again."

"I . . ."

"Your husband came here looking for you once. Many years ago. He came to my home, and I spoke with him."

"What?" I whispered. "I . . . Idris?"

He leaned back. "I didn't think I'd ever see you again."

What had The Now made my story into? I felt untethered. I was literally outside of the fabric of time. My first husband Idris had never stood there watching me walk into and out of our burning home after I'd been brutally raped by General Daib and the Nuru had destroyed our village. Idris had never rejected me and then shamefully turned as I walked away.

"The man was so confused," Obi said. "Ah, but that was long ago."

Was it? I thought. It only changed recently.

"Now is now," was all I said. "How are you, Obi?"

"Why are you sitting in a men's club?" he asked.

"Am I not allowed?"

"You've always had a habit of invading the spaces of men."

I laughed. "You know about that?"

"You're legend here. If people around here knew who you were, you'd have an entourage escorting you everywhere. Your nonsense has made Adoro 5 the wealthiest Adoro village. Will you stay?"

"Obi," I breathed. "Slow down. Can we just sit and drink?"

"I just . . . can't believe you're here. I've thought about you a lot over the years." He looked at his palm wine and took a sip. "I think of you often."

I narrowed my eyes at him. He looked ready to jump out of his skin. What was my presence doing to him? Obi and I had loved each other, and then I'd enchanted him during those last years when we were teens. Even after he married, I know he must have thought of me often. What did The Now do to his memory of me? What did my being outside of The Now, my being a sorceress do? I should have left him alone. I stood up. "I should go, Obi."

But I was also feeling destructive. This night was going to be like no other. I stepped over to him and leaned forward, taking his face in my hands. As I kissed him, I gently lifted a little out of myself, letting the kponyungo blaze. I settled back into myself as I parted his lips with mine and gently bit his tongue. I sucked his lower lip as I pulled away and then looked down into his astounded face.

"My . . . wife will . . ."

"Goodbye, Obi."

I strolled about the market until people began packing up in the late hour. Only a few would stay the entire night. Sellers of medicines, brews, and night creatures like bats and darkling beetles, palm wine, fried snacks, and torches. There was an old woman who called herself a seer. I'd walked by slowly, and she showed no interest in me, choosing instead to call over two young women walking by. I'd chuckled to myself.

Around ten o'clock, I decided to go to the hill that was now beside my old home. The lights inside were on. The hill gave a nice view of Adoro 5, yet it was not a place where anyone spent time. The only thing that grew here had died, a palm tree. I set my pack beside it and brought out and spread a small mat.

I'd sat here with Ting weeks ago. Now, I leaned my back against the dead tree. The last meal I'd eaten was two days ago, a day after I'd left Ssolu. I'd only had the few groundnuts the women had shared with me. And I'd expressed my milk three times today. Still, I wasn't hungry. I felt strong. But I was scared. I knew I could find it, but I had no plan. This was not the past or the future. This would happen in the present. There was no preparing.

I took some minutes to express milk from my breasts. There was enough to feed Sssolu and then some. I let it wet the ground at the base of the dead palm tree. I mixed it with the dry soil. Something would eventually grow here. I touched the piece of blue glass hanging from my neck. Dedan had given it to me just before we parted. I imagined that it gave me clarity. Dedan's Glass House had been his way of seeing through the veil. Through time and the times. I lifted it to my eye and peered through the blue. My eye landed on the place that had been home and now was not. "Sssolu, give me strength," I whispered. I let the necklace fall to my skin, exhaled softly, and shut my eyes. In those seconds, I mentally flew through all that Aro and Sola had taught me, all that I'd taught myself. I saw Dedan's face and felt Sssolu's destiny.

I rose from my body, flames billowing around me. I reached the top of the dead palm tree and several of the dry leaves ignited. Within moments the crown above my body was in flames. I roared and whirled, thinking of my daughter. I screamed her name as I whirled, whipping the warm air and extinguishing the burning palm tree crown. Ashes fell over my body, but I didn't stay to watch them settle or make sure none of them carried flame to burn my flesh.

I flew up high, until I could see Adoro 5 in its entirety. The silence and calm were sweet, and as I scanned the lands with my kponyungo's eye, I enjoyed the moment. I stayed up there for hours. Searching. And searching. And searching. Over the neighborhoods. In the streets. Outside the Paper House. In the markets. At the stables of the camel sellers. In the scrub brush between homes and buildings. Around the Adoro temple. Near schools. The fields where corn grew.

Nothing.

I remembered when I'd sensed The Cleanser. I had not had to do more than look. Smell. See. And I'd felt all this in Adoro 5 all the way from Jwahir. The Cleanser's presence snatched my senses and pulled me to it, regardless of my interest and unawareness. Nothing snatched my attention now. Nothing pulled me to it. The night was calm. And it was waning. The moon was barely a sliver, the wind lazy, the night cool. Had I somehow missed it? Maybe it had already come, chosen a child, and gone. I began to fret.

After another hour, about two hours before sunrise, I decided to fly even higher. I didn't know what else to do, and the idea of nearly leaving the Earth was somehow soothing. I flew so high that I could see the planet's curve. I turned to the South. Just for a moment. A distraction. Toward Dedan and Sssolu. Just for one moment, I wanted to look toward my family. Then I would look back down at Adoro 5 and hopefully finally spot The Cleanser and do to it what I came to do.

From so high up, the storm that hid and protected

Ssolu looked tiny. My kponyungo's eye could see in the darkness and so the brown, tan, yellow spiral of dust and sand was clear. I was about to turn back to Adoro 5 when I suddenly found I *couldn't*.

Because.

I blazed so massive that I must have looked like a miniature exploding star in the night to anyone awake in any of the Adoro villages. I was moving before I processed I was doing it. I couldn't help it. Three days on foot to Ssolu. Mere seconds as a kponyungo. And as I approached the storm, I flew low and plunged into it.

There are times when everything stands still. I've experienced this often now. We exist inside and outside The Now. We remember The Before. We understand so much and live with that knowledge. Sola once told me a little about how he moves. Coming and going. What I was experiencing just before I finally set eyes on The Cleanser must be what he experienced whenever he stepped out and stepped back in. There was a sweetness to it, a falling away.

I landed on my feet in the winds of Ssolu's protective dust storm. I stood there watching it . . . walk. It was tall, easily twice my height. Long legs. Long arms. Ramshackle garments. Brown. Dirty. Oily. Dusty. In many ways, it reminded me of those spirit creatures whose attack had eventually killed my father. Raffia hung from the collar of its long shirt and the cuff of its pants. Its pumpkin-sized head was coming and going like the sand of a dune, sliding and collecting without falling. Its back was to me, so I could not see its face. I couldn't tell you what it smelled like because we were in a dust storm.

As the wind didn't blow me away, it did not blow it away, either. It was heading to Ssolu for the only Osu-nu child in the village. My daughter Sssolu.

I realized my power early in life. From the moment I had the Call. I had unquestionable evidence of a . . . gift. Knowing what I know, I now wonder why The Cleanser never came for me. The witch took me that day when I was with my father and only because I'd thrown myself at it. I'd been so sure I would be fine. Then I sold the salt in the market of men for more than any man could sell it. As a child, as a girl. With confidence. Consistently, for years.

I began witching and soon, when I was witching, I became the kponyungo. Then I was raped and destroyed, but I still lived. I gave birth and raised a magnificent woman who changed the world. I demanded to be trained and was trained by magnificent sorcerers. They could not question what I was and how mighty I was. And so I took that moment to take on The Cleanser. And then, with no plan, I threw myself at it. My mind was empty. My slate was clean. I thought of nothing. I only acted.

Raging red kponyungo spirit. I'd done it before, as the masquerade had told me I had. To the sorcerer Daib, as his atonement. Yes, I knew exactly how to do this thing I needed to do. I was the color, smell and sound of fire. Just before I plunged into it, it turned. A chest of rags, dirt, ribbons that looked like flesh. And there was a stink: sulfuric, slick, damp, spoiled, the inside of a putrid cave.

Now I saw the face.

Sliding and slipping sands. No mouth. A crusted hole for a nose. The eyes like yawning maws, the sides drawn down, black ichorous sludge glistening from the edges. They widened, as I flew at it. I was a burning arrow, more final than the one that had pierced my father's sister's chest. I'd been wrong. Everything about it was wrong. This thing . . . it was an abomination.

"How can this be?" I whispered, shuddering with disgust.

I would have been afraid when I crossed over if I hadn't spent many years in the wilderness with the kponyungo. I didn't lose focus and it did not escape. I went right for it as I had gone for the thing inside Daib. And I set it on fire.

I once saw the woman whose name was Phoenix destroy the Earth. She decided to destroy everything. She decided to become the sun and wipe the slate clean. I will always hear her final thoughts in my consciousness, "Let them die. Let everything die." An incantation, strong juju. She wasn't a sorcerer, but she was. Now it was my turn to decide on something great.

I set eyes on it. And as it saw me, I felt something in my forehead burn.

"One of you. Time and time again," it said in its smooth, oily voice. "That is all I take. That is all who gives. And when they come back, are they not better?

It is not much to give, not much to suffer." It moved closer and I could see all that it was, a network of sticks, stones, and bones. A face made of sand. "Don't you want peace?"

I shook, realizing that it was trying to hypnotize me. Convince me. Change me, smooth me out. As it did with all the Osu-nu people it took. I pulled back, angry. Insulted. I reared up, fire, dust, and wind. I was a witch with only one way. I roared them at it, "I don't want peace with you . . . I WANT DESTRUCTION! I AM YOUR TROUBLE! YOUR DEATH!"

The Cleanser became all sharp things, sticks with stabbing tips, needles of stone, knives of sand. Its face was gone, except for what looked like long snaggled teeth.

"I am not afraid of death," I said.

"Maybe I will take you."

Its hand was around my neck before I even knew it could move. How could it grab me when I was spirit? It was pulling me down into the sand. Whatever was in my forehead blazed so brightly that for a moment, everything flashed white. It was like a chip of molten metal. I remembered that moment when Cat had touched my forehead. It had felt wet then. What had it been? Whatever it was, it had The Cleanser's attention as it pulled me down. It reached forward, gently, curiously, with its free gnarled and stick-like hand. I held myself still. *Wait,* I thought. *Wait. Hold.* Its hand was less than an inch from my face. I could see the flesh of it. It *was* alive. A living masquerade. A reversal. *Hold,* I thought again. *Wait.*

When it touched the light, there was the sound of a tiny bell. Just once. *Ting!* Then it pressed its fingers together like a vise on the light. To dig it out of me. The pain was blinding. I snarled with rage. Even now, it felt entitled to take. It had never been challenged. It had been taking and taking for so very long. Keeping my people unremarkable. For what reason? I didn't care. I took my chance.

I tore at it.

I tore it apart.

I took its life.

I *killed* it.

There must have been a part of it that blew away in the dust storm. I still wonder if the people of Ssolu found a piece of mask, a piece of shirt, some sticks. Or maybe everything just disintegrated and became more dust, feeding the storm that protected my family and the Vah people of Ssolu. What I did know was that when I came back into this story, there was a shock wave that was swallowed by the storm. I doubt anyone in Ssolu noticed it, except *maybe* Ssaiku and Ting. Maybe. I was in my human spirit form, and I no longer felt physical pain, but something was very wrong.

There are consequences to all juju. Some good, some bad, some just weird, some insignificant. This one was bad. I was wearing my flowing garments that moved with a sort of spirit wind. However, where my garments were usually soft and periwinkle in color, they were now shredded to rags, the edges burned. I pulled at them and more of the material crumbled away. I didn't understand. I was not in physical form. What did this mean? Horrified, I shifted into the kponyungo and was relieved when I felt and looked like myself. I flew back to my body and came within sight of it in seconds.

But I couldn't see my body. The palm tree was in flames.

CHAPTER 13

What I Know

The smell of burning flesh. Burning leaves, branches, and ashes had fallen on me. The fire had traveled halfway down the slender trunk. I was coughing when I returned to myself. My left leg and left arm were shrieking with pain where burning twigs had fallen on my skin. My forehead was wet, and there was a painful itchiness there. I touched it and when I brought my hand away, it was bloody.

"There's a woman up there!" someone shouted from the bottom of the hill. People were gathering. They weren't my concern. The group of creatures wearing dirty tattered garments standing yards away on the hill was my concern. They walked toward me, casually, like they had all the time in the world, as if it didn't matter whether I fled or not.

I jumped up and fled. I have shapeshifted before. Not completely, just parts of my body. That day when the waters flooded Jwahir, I changed my feet and hands to swim better. I could do small things like that and I didn't do it often. I couldn't change into a vulture and fly away as Aro and my daughter could. That was not the Mystic Point that was my natural talent. So I only had my legs, lungs and adrenaline.

I could run fast and jump high. I was tall with long powerful legs and I was in good shape. I had been travelling for nearly a year while pregnant. I was strong. I ran fast down that hill toward the house where I grew up that may or not remember me. There were three people standing before it, but there was light shining behind them, and it was dark. I couldn't see faces, but one of them was probably a man, the other two women. I made a sharp turn toward the road as one of them shouted, "Hey!" The man. The voice was familiar. Oh, it was so familiar. But I kept running. Whatever was after me, let them come after me. Only me.

That voice was so familiar.

I blinked away tears and ran up the road. I'd killed The Cleanser. I'd done it. The consequences were coming for me. I was running, but I knew what was coming for me did not worry about space or time. I understood what The Cleanser was, now. It was indeed an abomination. No masquerade should ever thrust itself into the living world as a living creature. It was all wrong. For so long, it had been all wrong. What its motive was, I will never know. But it was a cursed creature.

And just before I killed it, it touched whatever Cat had put in my forehead. Then it took it, ripping it out. I'd felt it, but I hadn't cared because I was tearing and tearing and killing. It took from me and died seconds later. Blood ran from my forehead and blurred my vision, my tears helped to keep my eyes clear. I slowed down when I reached the town square. There were still booths that were open, and a few people looked at me as I stood there wheezing, bloody and burned.

"Are you all right?" a young man carrying an armful of textiles asked. He looked more closely at me and shuddered, stumbling back.

I looked behind me up the road, and I could see them. They were filling the street, walking at a casual speed. I looked around quickly. North. South. Behind me East. Ahead to the West. I don't know why I decided what I decided next. I like to think it was my father's spirit, just as I like to think that the man at my childhood home was my father, alive and well. Yes, my father was on my mind. It was why I kept running. I did not want those spirit creatures who had returned because of The Cleanser's death to find my father a second time in The Now.

I fled South. Like he did that terrible day when they'd killed his family, I ran to my village's Adoro temple. It was on the outside of town, I wasn't far from it, I knew how to get there, if it was still there. I hoped the spirits following me wouldn't want to go inside it.

There is an Adoro temple in every Osu-nu village. It is generally believed that The Cleanser never visits there. Spirits and deities don't visit each other's places of worship. And if you are not Osu-nu, you'd be stupid to go there, even in The Now. It's a place for only us and I believe it always will be. The Adoro temple is always on the outside of town, it is the quiet heart of Osu-nu culture. The old word is "obi". If we are still Osu-nu, then the temple will still remain.

And there it was. As I ran to it, I felt such a sense of self and pride. This was exactly where I needed to be. The temple was always left alone. Someone would polish and dust it, make sure birds did not make it filthy. Maybe the overseer; I never knew. No one did. Regardless, few ever spent much time here. It was a quiet place whose existence gave everyone a sense of peace, but didn't require our presence. Only the most desperate came here. And in the night, only people like me.

The front door was painted red and drawn above it in black sweeping letters was, "Adoro 5." In small letters it said, "A good heart makes good people." When I stepped in, I froze. The wooden roof had caved in, the pieces of it piled to the left of the Adoro goddess statue. It looked like something that had happened years ago. The place was dusty with sand and dirt. Some birds shrieked and took to the sky, sending more dust and dirt in the air. Dedan would not have liked this place. It was made of heavy stone where he preferred clear glass. And it was crumbling and forgotten. No one came here, no overseer dusted it. I frowned, sadly wondering now if the Osu-nu were still the Osu-nu. And now that The Cleanser was dead, would this . . . who were we now?

"Dedan. Sssolu," I whispered. And I felt a little better.

I looked up at the red clay statue of the Adoro goddess. She stared at me with her intense gaze as she grasped her staff with the skull on top. I reached down and picked up one of the pieces of coal at her feet. I looked up and stared at myself in the large mirror behind her in the moonlight that was still somehow fully intact. I whimpered with dismay. My forehead was an open wound.

How am I alive? I wondered.

There were other smaller wooden statues in the temple. The walls were covered with white geometric shapes, their insides detailed with black lines that reminded me of nsibidi. None of this was juju. The Adoro temple was worship and respect paid to the deity that both enslaved *and* saved the Osu-nu people. It was mythology but there was deep mysticism in it. There was reach. There was a path to arrival. A sorcerer glowed and burned in a place like this.

I paused, hearing them outside. Yes, I was already surrounded. I rested my head against the cool stone wall, trying to calm my breathing. I looked at my shaking hands. I coughed, pulling a sliver of wood that had at some point dug into my left hand.

I wiped more blood and tears from my eyes and looked up at the sky through the open roof. I let out a calm breath. The sky was clear and full of stars. I stepped forward and stumbled as I stepped on the crumbled remains of one of the idols. There was the sound of things crunching and grinding beneath my feet as I turned. There was something large outside. I heard a whoosh.

I considered becoming the kponyungo. I could leave. I wasn't helpless. I wasn't trapped. But I'd decided this long ago. I would never abandon my body. Not for anything. Not even to save my spirit. My body was mine. One of my purposes was to care for it, protect it. Just as I had protected my children. So I stayed. And I looked up, right into its face.

By this time, I remembered. I knew what I'd see. It all made sense now. It still could take, even as it returned, in rage, to its most elemental form. My eyes never left it. All I could do, as I sat down hard on the stone ground in the crumbling Adoro temple was stare up into it.

Delicate and soft white. It unfolded like freshly washed cloth that was still a tiny bit wet as it dried in the sun. Maybe it was flesh, but something that was not alive didn't have flesh, did it? It unfolded and unfolded, revealing deeper and deeper layers. It was gigantic, filling the temple now, knocking over the Adoro statue, the smaller idols, nudging aside the collapsed roof. The remaining walls of the temple buckled.

I could not see the legion of spirits that surrounded the temple ruins because this creature that had once been The Cleanser, and for the first time in centuries was back to its true form, was filling everything. It was bigger than anything I could perceive. It was not alive. It was outside of life. It was an essence.

Finally, there was its face. It leaned over me. Wide fishlike lips, empty eyes. I was screaming. Maybe I had been screaming all along. There was blood pouring down my face, into my eyes, warm, wet, metallic. There was pain. It was awful. I felt a summit of pain, an itch, then a letting go. I gasped. Tightness in my chest. And then I was roaring and burning. I knew to draw one thing. I drew it with my mind. The juju for "flight." I'd always known it. Of the Mystic Points, the Mmuo Point was my strongest and this juju was one of its cornerstones. I thought of it now more as homage to myself than function. Still, it is powerful and always aware.

What I know is that a long time ago, I dreamed of leaving everything behind, walking into the desert, shedding my body in death and becoming the Alusi that my father was always sure lived in me. I'd then spend eternity wandering the desert. That distant dream, like my name, was my destiny.

I am a witch. The kponyungo. Fire, dust, and wind. I fly low over the sand dunes, the sun blazing above, the moon glowing in the same sky. Sacred place. Mystical place. Occupied place.

Onyesonwu has gone.

Dedan remembers.

Sssolu will create.

The path is clear now.

THE END